# Hebrides Tide

By
H H Inglis

First published in 2023



ISBN 978-1-7384880-1-8

For Richard and Tom and in memory of Debra

# Acknowledgements

This novella, or "noirling" as I like to think of it, is a 'Thank You' note for the rich vein of Scottish noir writing, which I have avidly read and enjoyed since moving to Edinburgh.

The exterior and part of the interior of Jamie's house on Old Hailes Road (an invented street) is loosely based on the Murphy House on Hart Street Edinburgh, the brilliant prize winning work of Richard Murphy Architects, to whom I am indebted for producing such an inspiring building.

I must give enormous thanks to my wonderful husband, Richard, and my wonderful son, Tom, who were my first readers and who gave me many invaluable comments. I would never have written the book without their encouragement and stalwart support.

Everything I write is for my beloved mother, Debra, who was a spellbinding story teller and instilled in both myself and my son from our earliest years a love of Scotland, especially the Hebrides.

# Table of Contents

# Part One

He kicked hard at the door. It juddered. He kicked harder. The rusted lock yielded and the door broke open in a hail of splinters. He could hear Catriona laughing in disbelief. He turned to her, squinting his eyes against the sun, and laughed too.

The light spooling into the dark interior drew them inside. They were hit by waves of dust and marine damp long entombed inside the boathouse. Towards the front of the boathouse near to the large wooden doors, he could see the shape of a boat tucked under a tarpaulin. Saying to himself 'I wonder if that is...' he began tugging at the tarpaulin. Catriona joined him and they dragged it off to reveal a small coastal sailing boat, still crisply painted orange and black with the sail wrapped like a mummy in the well of the boat. An outboard motor was attached to the rear.

'It's the Papa Westray' he exclaimed in delight. Memories flooded in. 'Do you remember those picnics in the Papa Westray?'

Catriona smiled 'Of course. I remember sailing to the little Isle of the Standing Stone. We played hide and seek in the shadow of the large stone and you proposed to me there. Bet you have forgotten that'.

He could not remember but he laughed anyway 'What did you say?'

She screwed up her face in fake concentration, saying 'I think I said 'Yes' but, as we were only ten years old, I won't hold you to it.'

In the gloom they could see the carcasses of four or five canoes stacked against the far side wall. Sprawling coils of rope impregnated with dried seaweed created hazards all over the floor. In the rear corner under the ladder stairs were rusting drums of diesel. Scattered around were twisted branches of bleached wood, punctured buoys and broken plastic toys which had been scavenged from the beach.

'Where does the ladder lead?' Catriona asked, pointing at the ladder stairs.

'Maybe a loft room of some kind, probably to store more boating tackle.'

He went over to scrutinise the ladder to see if it was intact and tentatively tested the bottom step. It looked quite solid and had clearly been securely fixed at the top. He cautiously began to climb up with Catriona following close behind him. He emerged into a room with high arched rafters which extended the full length of the boat house. Sun was streaming in through a window in the apex of the roof.

What greeted them was wholly unexpected and took their breath away. Three of the walls were covered by large painted panels. On the two long walls the paint had been delicately handled in tones of blue grey and silver from which emerged shadowy shapes of a forest fringing a ghostly lake. The waters of the lake rippled and shimmered from the reflective glow of a harvest moon painted in thick orange impasto. It was eerily beautiful and had a hypnotic effect upon Jamie. He felt for a moment he was there standing alone on the shore of the lake staring into the swirling depths of its icy waters. The forest trees of birch, spruce and aspen crowded round him, their branches almost brushing his neck. He could sense the timelessness of the forest stretching for mile after mile into an unimaginable infinity, constantly raked by bitter winds sweeping in from the Tundra plains. His imagination left him momentarily untethered. The words 'Always dance the orange' played round in his head. Catriona whispered in his ear 'Jamie, what have we stumbled on?' Jamie understood what she meant. It felt as if they had entered some mystical chapel or hushed sanctuary where speaking out loud seemed a defilement. Candles in glass jars placed along the walls added to the sense of a chapel.

In the centre of the room was a small bench made out of driftwood. There was no other furniture in the room. The bench was placed to face the painting which entirely filled the third wall. This painting was a complete contrast to the other paintings in style and mood. It was a crowded nativity scene. The figure dominating the centre of the scene was a seated Virgin dressed in a luminous blue robe. She had a beautiful, Botticelli shaped face which she inclined towards a smiling baby Jesus sitting on the edge of her lap. He was holding out his chubby arms to a kneeling figure of Joseph who was wearing a shabby leather jerkin; his lowered face obscured by a mass of tangled hair. What was unexpected was that the figures flanking the traditional biblical scene were not shepherds or kings but fishermen in their oilskins and crofters holding mattocks for cutting the peat.

Catriona was peering intently at the various characters thronging the scene. She suddenly cried out 'Jamie, look. I swear that's my father in his favourite Harris tweed jacket'.

Jamie stood close to the surface of the painting and scrutinised each of the faces. 'It is definitely your father and there are my grandparents,' he said, pointing at an elderly couple with happy smiles, who stood to the right of Mary.

They both spent the next few minutes taking it in turns to identify the various local characters who had peopled their childhoods: The Reverend MacCloud, the stern Minister, and his two bespectacled, school mistress daughters, Miss Cecily and Miss Jean; Mrs Bessie Dalbeith the matronly post mistress; Finlay McDougall, the lobster fisher and his two strapping sons, Davie and Will, and old Ben Gillespie, whose hilltop croft had the best view of the bay. There was a host of other familiar faces. Jamie was especially charmed by striking images of his grandparents, who were sweetly holding hands. Not only were the portraits good likenesses but they had captured the essence of their different personalities, Grandfather's excitability and Grandma's practical calmness.

Catriona clapped her hands in delight 'Look, there's you, me...and Isla and Finn.'

Towards the bottom right of the painting was a group of four children with skinny legs wearing baggy T-shirts, shorts and oversized sandals. Three of them were sitting in a huddle over a game of squares which the fourth, who was standing to their right, sideways on to the viewer, was marking out with a long stick in the sand. They were taking no notice of the nativity but were absorbed in their own world.

'How old would we have been there?' he asked as he scrutinised their younger selves.

'Seven or eight, maybe' guessed Catriona.

'These are really extraordinary portraits' he said, 'I wonder who on earth painted them?' He stepped back from the mural and scanning the whole scene, looked puzzled 'Someone is missing? Where is Miss May? There are Miss Cessie and Miss Jeanie, but I can't see Miss

May'. The three sisters had been inseparable, living their whole lives together in the Manse.

Catriona was not listening as she was still minutely examining the gang of four children. Isla's elfin face peeping out of her long silver hair was unmistakeable. You could feel Finn's ungainliness by the spiky awkwardness of his pose. She herself looked like a proper little urchin with a rag mop of black curls. In contrast, Jamie, the fourth figure, with his shoulder length light auburn hair and Grecian features, had the grace of Donatello's David.

'He always was a beautiful child' she said to herself. She stole him a glance. He had not lost that extraordinary grace in the way he held himself. He remained tall, long limbed and slender but his shoulders had now broadened. His finely chiselled features were handsome in a conventional way but carried a depth of character, a quality which had become more pronounced as he had grown older. His looks could have made him arrogant but he was the opposite, a blue eyed dreamer, who could suddenly turn on you a startlingly clear gaze, which drew you into his world of imagination. He was constantly animated by a stream of ideas, only his hands betraying his nervous energy by their restless, unselfconscious motion. His hair still flopped too casually into his eyes.

It troubled her that she still felt so wholly attuned to him. This was despite the anger she had felt towards him in her teenage years. She had so wanted to run free with him but found that he had placed her in a box with Isla and Finn under the category of 'childhood friends.' However hard she tried, there was no way she could claw her way out of the box. She partly blamed her moody teenage years on Jamie's indifference towards her. He failed to notice that she was growing up with deep feelings for him. She was unable to recover her natural equilibrium until she was well away from the island. University had been a fresh start for her and had finally put on end to her moping. There she had met Paul, who had loved and wanted her.

The light pouring through the window drew Jamie like a magnet and he was rewarded with a panoramic view. The perimeters of the window captured, like a camera obscura, the full sweep of the large bay, Bagh a Tomara, with the ragged peaks of the Torrenish mountains fringing its distant shore. As the sun was shining and there was little wind, the sea and the sky formed a mirror image of pure silver. Eilean na-h Fhada was the northernmost island of an archipelago off the north west coast of the Scottish Highlands, unspoilt and paradisiacal with its constant play of rain, rainbow and sun, a glittering jewel in the Hebridean crown.

'What a wonderful view to paint', he murmured to himself, 'Strange that the painter chose to paint an imaginary place of lakes and forests rather than this magical seascape'.

Catriona was looking closely at the Joseph figure. 'Jamie, there are some letters here. Can you make out them out?' she asked.

He went over to where she was standing and peered closely at a tiny area of paint which she was tracing with her index finger. Letters had been scratched into the paint along the bottom edge of the leather jerkin. He could make out an A and an R but the other letters were so faint as to be barely there. 'Aron or maybe Arna' he said tentatively. 'It must be the artist's name. Do you know of any local artist who may have used the boathouse as a studio?'

Catriona shook her head 'No but we can ask my father. As the local GP he knows every one. "the good and the bad from the cradle to the grave." as he puts it himself.'

'Whoever he was, he was one hell of a painter'. Jamie was musing out loud to himself, as he scanned the face of the Madonna. 'So sensuous, so tender...The way he painted her is ravishing.' He continued to stare at the painting, 'To paint like that the painter must have felt deeply'. He had a momentary flash of recognition as he gazed at the perfect oval face but it was lost almost immediately and he could not summon it back.

Catriona was looking round and said 'There's a radio or something in that corner'. She went over and picked up a bulky, oblong shaped object which she brought over to Jamie. It was an old fashioned tape recorder. He fiddled with the knobs but the batteries had long since worn down. He opened up the back of recorder and showed her that the batteries had begun to leak inside.

'What do you think this room was used for?' Catriona said.

'It looks like a chapel or some place of worship or maybe a place for meditation. It must have taken years to paint the panels.' said Jamie, 'They must have been painted in situ. It looks as if ship canvas was used rather than primed artist's canvas. What is clear is that these paintings were created by a painter of extraordinary power and passion.'

Jamie looked back at the swirling orange moon and suddenly the vibrant orange triggered a picture. It was a complete recall in his head of the picnic on the Isle of the Standing Stone, which had failed to materialise when Catriona had first mentioned it. Images now came vividly into his mind. He could see the two of them standing with the megalith looming over them, intimidating but companionable. Miss May came up to them and clasped their hands together. She softly repeated to them again and again like a mantra 'Always dance the orange.'He did not understand what she meant. He recalled being too frightened to ask. Miss May, always so gentle and kindly, had transformed into something slightly weird and out of control which he found unnerving. He remembered later asking his grandmother what the words meant. She said that she thought it was a quote from something, maybe a poem but she could not recall which. She told him that he was not worry because the words could only have been meant kindly. He had never thought of those words again until that day.

***

When Jamie had learnt that he had been named as an executor in Miss May's will, his first thought had been to refuse and leave it to the lawyers. His workload in Edinburgh, a good six hours away from the island was, he believed, a reasonable and proper excuse. Then he thought of Miss May with her round, kindly face, her white wispy hair always escaping from her unravelling bun. He recalled her infinite gentleness and patience with him as a child. She loved children, always devising little parties with home baked cakes and expeditions in the Papa Westray. When he was three or four years old and staying with his grandparents for a month in the summer, he would go once a week to the Manse for tea with his grandmother. The three sisters would be sitting in the conservatory, deep in their rickety, green wicker chairs.

Miss May would disappear for a time and then return with two large plates, one heaped with lamb and mint sauce sandwiches, their crusts neatly removed, and the other, a pretty china plate crowned with a sponge cake filled with pineapple and cream, baked particularly for him. He loved her sensitive playing of Chopin or Beethoven on the manse piano, which he could hear through the open windows. Her soaring chords mingled with the chatter of the crows in the fir trees guarding the Manse. These sounds formed the magical backdrop to his summers.

The fact was, he told himself, that she had chosen him as her executor. When he had sat down, thought about it and talked it through with his partner, Ellie, he felt shallow in wanting to shirk this responsibility. He just knew that his grandparents would have thought less of him if he had and that mattered to him. Nevertheless he did wonder why she had chosen him. In his view, Isla and Finn would have been far better candidates being so firmly rooted to the island.

He was thinking about this, when, shortly after his arrival on the island, he walked up a steep track marking out the path to the Manse in the cropped turf. The Manse was perched on the brow of the cliffs which plunged precipitously down into the broiling waves washing their feet. Tarkavay House was a square Georgian building dressed in dark, grey stone. In the traditional way the building turned a blank wall to the wide vista of the bay below. The Georgian builders had been more concerned with the practicalities of protecting the property from the savage winds which often ravaged the island. As it was, the elegant, sash windows, which were the symmetrical face of the house, rattled precariously even in a slightest of breezes. The wind had dictated not only the orientation of the house but also the planting of a windbreak of fir and birch trees which stood like sentinels to the side and the rear of the property. The black, forbidding front door was flanked on either side by terracotta pots of tumbling scarlet fuchsia, which did much to soften the approach. Fixed to the centre of the door above the letterbox was a small copper plaque, which had gone green with age but on which you could still discern the name 'Reverend Doctor Caleb MacCloud'.

Jamie took out the large old fashioned key and with some difficulty, as the lock was stiff, opened the door. Contrary to the practice on the island, the Manse had been locked. This had been felt to be fitting until the executors had carried out their inspection. He had arranged to meet Catriona, his co-executor, but she had texted to say that she would be late. So he decided to take a first look round on his own.

A long stone paved hallway led from the door into the dark recesses of the house. He knew his way round the ground floor of the property, as he had visited many times as a child. At the end of the corridor it turned left towards the wooden spindled staircase which spiralled its way upwards through the two upper floors of the house. As he climbed, he bypassed the first floor which had been the Reverend MacCloud's domain containing his bedroom and library. He felt uncertain about intruding into the Reverend's inner sanctum by himself. So he left those two rooms until Catriona arrived.

Jamie carried on climbing to the second floor. This floor had a long, narrow landing with a rush plaited runner which ran along its length. Three doors led to each of the daughters' bedrooms. As he popped his head into each one, he noted that they were all sparingly furnished. The rooms had in common a single iron bed, a stool as a bedside table and a small pine wardrobe. The rooms had small windows, which looked onto the firs at the rear of the property, the close proximity of which made the rooms dark and enclosed. By each window was a small wooden table, more a console, which appeared to serve as a desk. A plain wooden chair was tucked underneath. No mirrors. No paintings. Just plain whitewashed walls. The only concession to comfort was the little white and black rag rug alongside the bed. Nevertheless two of the rooms at least managed to yield up a few clues as to the sisters' distinctive personalities.

Miss Cecily was the eldest sister and was always known as Miss Cessie. She had been the headmistress and sole teacher of the primary school on the southern tip of the island. This had catered for about a dozen of the crofters children. She must have had an iron constitution as she cycled in all weathers across the island. She was a conspicuous figure in her capacious cream mackintosh and an incongruous yellow southwester. She was a large, angular woman with a forbidding helmet of steel grey hair. Her height made her look imposing and a little frightening to new recruits to the school. Although a strict disciplinarian, the children quickly learnt that her bark was worse than her bite. Despite her social diffidence with adults, she earned the children's respect by her scrupulous fairness and won their love by the deep generosity of her spirit.

Jamie knew her softer side first hand. She shared his grandfather's passion for angling and the two of them would often spend a Saturday afternoon fishing the burns which criss-crossed the island. During the summer holidays she would occasionally take Jamie out in the Manse's old Ford for a day's fishing. Her fishing base was an old, battered caravan, which she kept in the field beside the Huish burn where it joined forces with Otta Burn to form a deep peat coloured pool. A solitary rowan tree defiantly grew at an acute angle on the bank of the pool. She was infinitely patient in showing Jamie how to tie the gossamer silk flies to the line. She would demonstrate to him the skilful overarm flick required to place the lure in the right spot in the running water to tempt a passing, gullible trout. Although he tried very hard, he rarely caught a fish bigger than a baby trout. He would carefully untangle the fish from the hook and throw it back into the water, saying to himself 'for another day'.

Jamie looked briefly in her bedroom. Although, on the surface, a clone of the other bedrooms, what distinguished it was her favourite fishing rod which was propped against the wall to the left of the wardrobe. Nestled underneath it was her old green canvas fishing bag, which he knew contained all her exquisitely fashioned flies. He made a note to himself that he should come back and rescue these, as he was sure that she would be delighted to think of him using them, perhaps with better success than he had as a boy. He was drawn to the muddle of books on her desk which were mostly practical books about fishing and gardening and a charming book of botanical drawings.

The bedroom next door belonged to Miss Jeanie. She was the briskly efficient middle daughter who ran the father's household like clockwork. She was somewhat stout but was always immaculately turned out in tweed suits, the colours of moss and purple heather. She was never without practical, sturdy brown brogues. She was short sighted and wore round tortoiseshell glasses, which gave her the air of an intense academic. Like her elder sister, she was a school mistress and taught at the local senior school in the inland village of Carruish, which Catriona, Isla and Finn had attended. All lessons were in Gaelic. Isla and Finn were from Gaelic speaking island families and Gaelic was spoken at home. When Jamie first met them, their few basic English words sounded heavy and clumsy in their mouths and funny to his ears. Catriona on the other hand was bilingual as she spoke to her father in English at home. Although her father had been born and bred on the island of Dorcha, he only ever mastered a smattering of Gaelic, enough to speak to his Gaelic speaking patients.

Underneath Miss Jeanie's somewhat austere, prim appearance there bubbled away a real passion for the Gaelic, which she was able to instil in her pupils with her calm determination. They all adored her. She never shouted or employed anger in order to discipline them. All it took, so he had been told, for her to steady her class was to raise her right eyebrow in faint disapproval. An immediate silence would descend; no pupil daring to breathe. Although he was never her pupil, the love the others felt for her had rubbed off on him and he always thought of Miss Jeanie with great affection.

It was consequently no surprise to Jamie to see on her desk a neat row of books tucked under the window. He went over and browsed the titles of the books. There was, given she was a daughter of the Manse, the inevitable bible with a thick looking commentary next to it. There was also a well thumbed Gaelic dictionary and grammar, a paperback of Sorley Maclean's 1943 collection 'Dain do Eimhir' and a selection of Sir Walter Scott's novels including her favourites 'Rob Roy' and 'The Heart of Midlothian'. Seeing the titles sparked a delightful memory of an occasion when Miss Jeanie had joined one of her sister's picnic expeditions. She kept them so spellbound as she read from her 'Rob Roy' in her deep sonorous voice that they almost forgot Miss May's waiting chocolate cake.

He closed the door on that happy memory and moved down the corridor to Miss May's bedroom. This shared the same sparse furnishings as the others. He imagined that her room would also give up glimpses of her more vibrant inner life. His first look round the bleak room was, however, not encouraging. Save for the Bible and a prayer book, there were no other telling books. There was a simple brown earthen ware jug, which he thought would probably have contained the wild flowers she loved to pick. He noted that a patchwork quilt made up of paisley squares covered her bed. This at least brought some colour and life to the room. Her sisters had nothing more than dark plaid blankets. He was perplexed that she had left so little trace of herself. She was the youngest of the sisters and, as far as he knew, had never worked. She was a clever cook, so his grandmother said. She brought subtle flavours with her ingenuous use of herbs and spices to the frugal ingredients which her father insisted were the only proper fare for a Manse. Her baking skills were a legend on the island. Jamie had always thought of Miss May as the romantic sister with a dreamy view of the world. Unlike her sisters' short neat hair, Miss May wore her long white hair in a bun. She tried to keep it in place with a tortoiseshell comb but pins spewed out wherever she went. As a result the bun was always on the verge of erupting from the comb. She rejected her sisters' pragmatic knee length skirts, preferring to wear long navy blue linen skirts. She always had a paisley scarf wrapped loosely round her neck save, of course, on Sundays. There was, however, nothing remotely romantic in the room and he felt strangely disappointed. It somehow felt important to him to find something of the essence of the Miss May he knew, some tangible mark but the room gave no hint of her personality.

He was suddenly surprised by the door of her wardrobe swinging open. A flotilla of large moths with orange powdery wings sailed out the wardrobe and slowly circled the room. They then flew to the window and began to batter themselves against the glass. Jamie found this frantic fluttering unbearable and hurried to open the window to release them. He watched them fly away, keeping a tight formation until they reached the pines, where they scattered and disappeared. The appearance of the moths had unsettled him and a dark melancholy swept over him. As he left Miss May's bedroom, he was weighed down by the thought that life left so few traces.

He was descending to the first floor when he heard the front door open and Catriona's tentative 'Hello'.

He shouted 'I'm upstairs. I'll come down' and he started down the flight of stairs from the first floor to the hallway.

On greeting, they hugged one another stiffly in the flagstone hallway. Catriona said 'Long time, no see. Sorry I am late but I have brought a thermos of coffee as a peace offering and so shall we start with coffee'.

'Great idea' said Jamie 'I've just had a look in the sisters' bedrooms. It was all a bit depressing. I can't imagine anyone wanting to spent much time there. So a coffee will cheer me up.'

They made their way to the conservatory and sank into the green wicker chairs, which had grown brittle after years in the sunlight. While they were drinking the coffee, Jamie mentioned how surprised he was at being made an executor. Catriona was also perplexed as to why she had been chosen. Like Jamie, she had felt the strong pull of obligation, despite her full life in Glasgow. Her partners in the Glasgow Medical Centre where she worked had been grudging, she said, in granting her the time away. Her husband, Paul, had been protective, not wanting her to take on more responsibility. Her old obstinacy had, however, taken hold in the face of all the objections and had propelled her to the island. An added bonus was that it gave her the chance to see her father.

Fortified by coffee they decided to tackle the first floor, Reverend Doctor MacCloud's rooms. His bedroom was tiny. It only just fitted a double bed and a narrow chest of drawers. There was no rug to soften the wooden floor. When they opened the door of his study, they gasped at the contrast. His book filled study was enormous. It was by far the biggest room in the house. His book shelves were stuffed full of grey buckram books, largely of sermons, hymns and biblical commentaries with maps of the Holy Land. Somewhat incongruously Jamie noticed that on the topmost shelf there were the collected works of John Buchan. Jamie liked to think of the old Reverend having a sneaky weakness for 'The Thirty Nine Steps' and out of curiosity stretched up to pick the book off the shelf. On the frontispiece there was an inscription in spidery, faded black ink, saying 'To Caleb, from Minnie, February 14th'. Jamie realised that these books must have been a gift from the Reverend's wife in the early years of their marriage. She had died relatively young, a few years after the birth of Miss May. Perhaps the presence of these books showed that in his private life he had had a mellow side to his character which he kept well hidden from his congregation. Jamie placed the book carefully back on the shelf.

***

It was after their reconnoitre of the Manse that they had decided to investigate the Boathouse, although it was some distance from the house. The western coast of the island was an intricate series of bays and headlands with narrow, penetrating sea lochs and black rocks shattered by the pounding seas. The Boathouse had been built on Rubda na Loinn, a ridge of land which jutted into Tomara Bay. From the main double doors ran a narrow slipway which sloped at a gentle angle towards the sea. The waves slopped over the last quarter of the slipway. The Boathouse belonged to Tarkavay House but no one was sure who built it or when. It was an unusual appurtenance to a Manse but, as children, they did not question the history. Canoes were their only means of exploring the turquoise, dancing waters of the smaller sea lochs. So they were simply happy to have access to the Boathouse canoes.

Having made their discovery in the Boathouse, Jamie and Catriona were anxious to talk to Catriona's father to see if he knew anything about the paintings and the painter. They left by the broken side door and began to walk round the extreme edge of the bay, allowing the lapping waves to chase them and periodically submerge their sandals in a rush of cold water. The sand was rippled with thin slicks of water between the shallow ridges. It was so yielding that their feet sank deeply at every step, leaving a momentary imprint, which instantly filled with water and disappeared, leaving no trace. They laughed together at the comical sight of three or four sanderlings racing on their tiny legs along the edge of the waves in their search for small crustaceans. Catriona could not resist stopping every few yards to pick up what she called "her treasures", shells and sea glass, half buried in the sand, which had been exposed by the low tide.

'I love beach combing at low tide', she said,' as you never know what secrets the waves have covered'.

Wet seaweed was spread like the tangled hair of a Medusa across a scatter of rocks which usually lay hidden beneath the waves. Every time Catriona stooped for 'treasure,' Jamie inhaled deeply, savouring the pungent scent of the sea.

'Look' cried Catriona 'There's a jelly fish!' They paused to peer down at the gelatinous circular shape, the size of a small plate, with its purple dye spreading out like tendrils. 'Ugh, I hate jelly fish' shuddered Catriona. They counted another four jelly fish stranded on the sand and one floating in the waves. It was like gossamer, billowing out and deflating. Jamie was taken by its delicate beauty.

A hundred yards from the Boathouse they made their way past an old stone smokehouse. At its side were the remnants of the poles from which the web of salmon nets had hung in the days when the salmon and lobster boats set sail daily from the little jetty. This had protruded proudly into the bay like a finger pointing the way to the Atlantic. Jamie only knew it from old photographs. It had long since crumbled into the sea leaving just a scattering of boulders to mark where it had been. Overlooking the remains of the jetty was a row of eight traditional whitewashed cottages with grey slate roofs. They huddled together under the high cliffs with their columns of basalt towering above them like a phalanx of giants. The cottages constituted the tiny village of Cearra.

Dr Fergusson owned two of the cottages at the eastern end of the row. He lived in the first cottage and used the second as his surgery and as a tiny dispensary. Maddie Henderson, the nurse, lived in the top cottage with her young family. They were recent and welcome arrivals on the island. Her three young children, Fergus, Zachary and Ishbel, had made up the numbers at the local primary school, which had been teetering on the edge of closure. Dr Fergusson and Maddie were the only health professionals on the southern part of the island.

The sun was low in the sky as they approached the cottages. Catriona swung open the weathered door of the first cottage, which led into a dark hallway. A miscellany of bulky coats, scarves, woollen hats and fishing bags hung from pegs on the wall with a neat row of rubber and walking boots tucked underneath. Catriona shouted out 'Dad, I've brought Jamie' as they both took off their coats and struggled to find a space on the pegs. Catriona placed her collection of shells and sea glass on the hall table. A shout came from one of the inner rooms 'Put the kettle on, Cat'. With a nod of her head to Jamie, Catriona disappeared through the door at the end of the hallway which led into the kitchen. The door on the left, half way down the hallway, was open. Jamie went in.

The room had a low beamed ceiling and Jamie found himself slightly stooping. The walls were of stone and the floor was made up of flagstones which had been softened by an ancient, worn Turkey rug. Two heavy Minty chairs with wide wooden arms, well upholstered in a faded red and green kilim, sat either side of a large stone fireplace, in which a log fire was burning and giving off a welcoming glow. Dr Fergusson was ensconced in the chair to the right of the fire and he waved Jamie to the chair on the left. Dr Fergusson was in his late sixties. He was immaculately turned out in a brown tweed suit enlivened by a lovat green moleskin waistcoat. He still had a full head of hair, of which he was secretly proud, though it had now turned from raven black to a foxy silver grey. What defined him as a character was his deep sense of faith and his unstinting service to his community. He remained as sharp as a whip and was an inexhaustible fountain of local knowledge. He was always saying that he was past his sell-by-date as a GP but the islanders would not countenance any talk of his retirement.

As Jamie lowered himself into his chair, Dr Fergusson echoed his daughter's earlier words 'Long time, no see, Jamie'.

Jamie responded with a shrug 'Pressure of work. It is not easy building up the practice. I have to take on a lot of small projects which I would not necessarily choose. But at least they get my name known and pay the wages. You wait, there's a big one just waiting round the corner... well so I hope'. Jamie laughed. He had always found it easy to talk to Dr Fergusson, who was a good listener. They settled down to a relaxed conversation about how the islanders were faring in the difficult economic times.

Catriona came bustling in with a circular metal tray, on which steaming mugs of tea were nestled together with a plate of home baked shortbread. Jamie and Dr Fergusson took a mug each and helped themselves to one of the shortbreads. Catriona sat on the squashy sofa opposite the fire. No sooner had she sat down than she launched herself into the story of their discovery in the Boathouse. Dr Fergusson sat quietly, sipping his tea, as her tale unfolded.

When she had finished, he bent down and vigorously prodded the logs with an iron poker, which caused the flames to fizz and leap higher in the grate.

'Well' said Catriona, a little impatiently 'Did you know about the paintings in the Boathouse? Do you know who Aron is?'

Dr Fergusson sat back comfortably in his chair and said teasingly 'Always two questions at once. Will you never learn patience? Well, the answer to the first is 'No' and the answer to the second in 'Yes'.'

Catriona and Jamie responded simultaneously 'Who is he?'

Dr Fergusson said 'It's at times like this, I could do with my old pipe, because it is quite a long story. His first name was Arvo, not Aron. His full name was Arvo Kusk. He was an Estonian, not a Russian as everyone believed. As far as I could gather, he had led an itinerant life as a child. His parents were members of a minority Eastern Orthodox congregation. His father was one of the specialist carpenters, who used to travel around repairing wooden chapels scattered in forests and along the Rivers Narva and Emajogi. By the time Arvo was an adolescent, he had lost both parents. I don't know in what circumstances...'.

He paused to take a sip from his mug before he went on. 'If I remember rightly, during the Second World War he was conscripted by the Russians into a Soviet Rifle Corp. As the German army reached Estonia in the early

1940s, he deserted, as did many other Estonians, only to find himself conscripted again in 1943, this time by the Germans into a newly formed Waffen-SS Brigade. He was sent to the front, first in Russia and then in France, where he was captured by the British. He was shipped out to England as a prisoner of war. He was sent up to Scotland and placed at Tarkavay House to work in the kitchen garden. He decided to stay at the end of the war. I asked him why, when he had the chance to go home. He said that there was no home for him in Estonia, which had been re-annexed as part of the Soviet Union. He had finally found a peaceful sanctuary, here on Eilean na-h Fhada, where he was always treated with kindness. He was my patient for over forty years for a chest condition, a consequence of the war. It took me all of that time to overcome his reticence about himself. He always struck me as an interesting, intelligent man. He was courteous in an old fashioned, gentlemanly way and deeply private. He only volunteered this outline of his life to me as a kind response to my insatiable curiosity.'

As he paused, Catriona jumped in with 'So Arvo is Ivan, the MacClouds' gardener?'

Dr Fergusson let out a long sigh and then placed his mug on the little wooden table at the side of his chair.

'Until now I have always respected his privacy and regarded what he told me as confidential between the two of us...rather like a priest treats a confession.' He hesitated for a moment before adding 'Now he is no longer here, I don't suppose I am breaching any confidence. Actually, it feels good that he should now take his proper place in the island's history.'

His daughter interjected 'But did he ever tell you that he was a painter and did you know about the murals in the boathouse?'

Dr Fergusson laughed and said 'Two questions at once again. Well, the answer to both is 'No'. As I said he was a very private man and he never mentioned anything about painting to me. Nor, come to think of it, did any of the Miss MacClouds. I guess one of them must have given him permission to paint in the Boathouse. I can't see the Reverend condoning such a thing. Anyway, my curiosity has been piqued and, if you don't mind, I am going to take a look at the paintings first thing tomorrow morning. You say, there is a portrait of me,' he said and shook his head, laughing to himself.

Jamie had been looking at a trio of tiny watercolours, which were facing him on the wall. Each was no more than three inches by two inches surrounded by a cream mount and a plain light oak frame. Intrigued he got up to have a closer look. They were in a soft, impressionistic style and depicted views of Bagh a Tomara and the Isle of the Standing Stone.

'Who painted the watercolours?' he turned to Dr Fergusson to enquire.

'Delightful, aren't they. They were gifts from the MacCloud sisters. My guess is that one of the sisters painted them. In many cottages on this part of the island you will see similar tiny watercolours, all gifts from the sisters'.

As he went back to his seat, it occurred to Jamie that the views of Bagh a Tomara in the watercolours were strikingly similar to the spectacular views from the Boathouse window.

Later that same evening, Jamie found himself again comfortably settled, this time into a deep sofa, the colour of burnt orange and moss green. The glow of another crackling log fire gently warmed his face. As it was late summer, the Highland nights were drawing in at a pace, dusk marching with reckless eagerness into night. Finn towered over him as he handed him a glass of Talisker, correctly predicting as he did so 'You will not be needing water'.

In the background he could hear Isla happily singing a Gaelic song as a lively accompaniment to the clatter of dishes in the kitchen. The children had settled in bed after Jamie had read a bedtime story to them. As he was doing so, he realised he was a little jealous of the domestic bliss his childhood friends exuded in their small but cosy cottage. The cottage was perched on top of the cliffs which overlooked the bay and the row of cottages below. It had been the watchman's cottage where the early nineteenth century excise man had lived and kept watch on the fishing boats to make sure that their cargo was fish and not contraband whisky.

Jamie remembered how it had been Finn and Catriona who had provided the steady ballast to their childhood dreaming, whilst he and Isla had been the drifters with their heads in the clouds. Jamie often wondered whether Isla, with her long silver hair, would vanish like a water nymph into the waves of some magic lake. Finn too had felt an instinctive need to protect this fragile, fairy creature. Finn, in contrast, had always been a caricature of the 'clumsy but gentle' giant, growing too tall too quickly. His uneasy overgrowth had made him stoop a little and hide his huge hands behind his back. Yet he could do anything with those hands. He kept them all entertained as children by manufacturing swords and shields from any old bits of cardboard. He created a shelter for them just from a few branches of of brush wood. As an adult, he still loved to tinker with bits of wood and bobs of machinery. He had added magnificently to his type casting by growing a flaming red beard. 'In honour of his Viking ancestors', he said. He would sit his twins, Esme and Fraser, on his lap and let them run their fingers through his beard whilst he growled at them like a bear and they wriggled with happiness.

There was an inevitability about Finn and Isla marrying as soon as they could. As the twins and then baby Lachlan came along, he had watched Isla transform from a water nymph into a capable mother goddess, her long silver hair now neatly braided. They were hefted to the land like the ubiquitous black highland sheep which dotted the hills and, together, they formed the bed rock of life on the island. Isla ran the mobile library and taught Gaelic once a week. Finn was the 'go to 'man for fixing leaky roofs, dodgy boilers and derelict tractors and an expert in rebuilding dry stone walls. He was a fine fiddler and accompanied Isla's Gaelic singing on a Saturday night at the community hall, a shed of corrugated iron behind the smokehouse.

Catriona, or Cat as they all called her, had been the tomboy of their childhood quartet, always with scratched knees and tousled hair. She had a Siamese cat's green flecked eyes, which could dart with sudden anger. She was a wild child, a risk taker who could climb any tree or crag without a backward glance. She careered along the winding island roads on her old Raleigh bike like a dynamo with her hair streaming in the wind. She could also be stubborn and was the only one who challenged his plans for an adventure as too tame.

She had realised her childhood dream of qualifying as a doctor. Her wild hair was now trimmed, collar length and styled, which matched her elegant but understated dress sense. Her face had narrowed and her features had sharpened into sculptured, high cheek bones which she emphasised with a touch of blusher. She was skeletally thin, which Jamie did not think suited her. He always associated her dramatic weight loss during her teenage years with a change in her personality. She had transformed from a happy go lucky child to a prickly adolescent with cropped, punk hair. It was as if she was wilfully smashing the bottle in which he kept his childhood memories and then using the broken shards as a weapon against him.

As a non islander, Jamie was, in theory, the outsider but, in practice, had always found himself warmly included by the other three. From an early age he had stayed during the summer months with his grandparents at their beach cottage, Lur Beag, and so in a sense had grown up with them all. When their own games were flagging from repetition, his arrival in the summer holidays brought fresh ideas. He would fuel their imaginations with tales of adventure and legends of heroic deeds. Under his direction, they enacted the Trojan War on the beach or explored for pirate treasure in rock pools or hunted for giant raptors in the dunes. Outside of the summers on the island he was a bookish child.

Those summer months were a time of magic for Jamie and, although he had always lived on the mainland, he felt as if the island was his true home. He had inherited the cottage from his beloved grandmother, Deborah. She was tiny in stature but packed an energetic punch. She had a ferocious intellect which she tempered with a special warmth, which had been a source of great comfort to him as a child. His ability to weave a yarn came entirely from his grandmother who was a spellbinding storyteller. From his earliest years, she had imbued in him a love of the Highlands and its rich, turbulent history. Her gift to him was a romantic sense of belonging. She had emotionally planted his roots in the island's soil and he remained under its spell, enchanted by its spirituality and its contemplative people. His spirits always lifted when he heard the Gaelic, even though he understood little of the language, save for a few words of a lullaby. His grandmother would sing this lullaby to him, as he was falling asleep. Her soft singing voice would fill his dreams with the sound of the waves on the shore and the 'strong screech of seagulls and the gathering of cockle shells.'He had also inherited his grandmother's second sight, an uncanny clairvoyance with flash backs and flash forwards. These lightening bolts of insight unnerved him as a child. Out of the blue he would see in his mind's eye a fleeting but vivid picture in heightened focus. It was unsettling when the scene in his head was re-enacted shortly afterwards in real time. These visions were random and of no practical use that he could see. Nevertheless it made him uneasy that he was not entirely like other people. As he grew older he tried to ignore these brief flights as just fancy.

His grandfather, Joseph, had been a leading architect in Scotland and the beach cottage, Lur Beag, had been a cutting edge, modernist design in the 1960s. His grandfather was always fizzing with big ideas, yet always gentle and big hearted. He had seemed tall to Jamie as a child but he was probably only five foot ten.

He had the typically Scottish ruddy complexion and thick, fiery ginger coloured hair which he kept until the day he died. A volcanic fury could suddenly erupt from him out of nowhere, only to dissipate in seconds and be instantly forgotten. His wife would frequently shake her head at him, but always with a broad smile. They laughed a lot together. Watching his grandfather creating extraordinary designs on his old drawing board had fuelled Jamie's love of architecture. His grandfather had encouraged his interest. There was always a stack of interesting architecture books by his bed in the cottage.

As an architect, Jamie had a head start living in the Edinburgh New Town, where he was surrounded by the well ordered spaces and classical proportions of Georgian housing at its best. Recently he had been so fully engaged in starting up his architectural practice in Edinburgh that his visits to the island had become fleeting. Recognising this, he had arranged informally with Finn and Isla that they could use the cottage for a holiday rental business. With a growing family, the money they made from the holiday business was proving a helpful supplement to their income. It made Jamie feel that he was not neglecting his cherished legacy by leaving the cottage empty for months at a time. He was also doing something useful for his friends, which his grandparents would have approved.

As Finn handed him the dram, he said 'Catriona just phoned to say that she was running late. She's been helping out her father at the evening surgery'.

'Even when she was a wee thing, she wanted to be a doctor like her Dad ' said Jamie. 'Have you met her husband, Paul. He's a doctor too, isn't he?'

'An orthopaedic surgeon, who works all hours for the NHS, according to Cat. He won't take private patients as a matter of principle He's a good bloke with a keen nose for a whisky and a great sense of humour...probably needs it working for the NHS,' Finn said with a grin.

'He's a bastard' came the damning verdict from the kitchen.

Jamie shouted through to Isla 'Wow. That's harsh coming from you.'

Isla popped her head round the door and said with a vehemence, which took him by surprise, 'He's making our Cat very unhappy. She desperately wants a child. He'd initially been as keen, but he's suddenly changed his mind. Now he's absolutely adamant that he doesn't want to be a father.'

Finn shook his head and gently remonstrated with her, 'Isla, they're both busy doctors in Glasgow. It is not our business. Anyway, Catriona will be here any minute and we don't want to upset her.'

Jamie was genuinely taken aback at the unprecedented sharpness of Isla's tone and even more by the uncharacteristic spasm of marital disharmony. When he first got to the island and had picked up the keys for his grandparents' cottage, Isla had warned him that 'Catriona was not herself' but there had no been time to ask the details. He began to understand when he had met up with Catriona at Tarkavay House. He could see straight away something was wrong, a haggard look about her eyes, but he was at a loss as to how to broach it with her. They had lost that ease of communication which they had as children. He knew that if he tried to intrude on her privacy, he would soon feel the sharp edged hackles of her resentment.

The conversation abruptly halted when the front door swung open and Catriona bustled into the room, shedding her coat and apologising profusely at the same time. 'Sorry, sorry I'm late everyone. Dad really ought to retire. It's getting too much for him.' She slumped down next to Jamie on the sofa. Finn handed her a glass of whisky which she gulped down before shouting to Isla in the kitchen, as if continuing an earlier argument, 'Don't start. You know I can't take over from Dad. My life's in Glasgow with Paul.'

Isla emerged from the kitchen carrying a large steaming casserole dish. She motioned with her head for them to sit at the table. The table had been made by Finn from an old farmhouse door which he had stripped and oiled so that it kept its rustic charm. The wooden chairs round the table were different shapes and sizes, but the heights were cleverly evened out by cushions of differing depths, all of which were covered in a willow leaf pattern. Over the backs of the chairs were sheep skins in varying shades of brown, grey and white. Isla placed the dish on a cork mat in the centre of the table and they all instinctively leant forward to smell the delicious aroma as she removed the lid.

'Rabbit stew' she announced and proceeded to ladle out generous proportions. 'Get the red wine would you' she said to Finn, who leapt to his feet and disappeared into the kitchen. They could hear the pull of the cork and then Finn re-emerged brandishing a bottle saying 'We should leave it to rest for a while but maybe I'll just pour'. Twinkling tea lights and little jam jars filled with wild flowers on the table gave a festive feel to the proceedings.

'This is the first time we have all been together for...

something like six years', said Finn, 'So I think it calls for a toast. Here's to Us.'

They clinked glasses and all in unison cried 'To Us!' Then it was heads down as they tucked into the rich stew and helped themselves to crusty rolls, which Isla had baked fresh that afternoon.

As Finn was pouring out second glasses of wine, the conversation turned to the mysterious Arvo.

Catriona said 'It's obvious when you think about it. He was the one with access to the boathouse but he gave no hint that he painted. We all thought of him as a gardener.'

'And everybody knew him as Ivan. I'd never heard the name Arvo' added Finn.

'Where did the name Ivan come from?' asked Isla.

'He had a Russian sounding accent and was given the nickname 'Ivan', which stuck, I suppose, and 'Arvo' got lost along the way', said Catriona, 'I gather he was too unassuming to correct anyone and over time he just accepted that he was Ivan. My father asked him once whether it bothered him and his response was that 'It was a lot better being called Ivan than Fritz'. I guess no one would be keen to be known as a member of the SS'.

There was a silence. As he had been listening, Jamie had a clear picture of Ivan. Even in his old age, he stood tall with no hint of a stoop. This was despite his years of endlessly digging and hoeing in the kitchen garden. He habitually wore a heavy, knitted jumper over a faded denim shirt and a dark brown, armless leather jacket which, due to long use, was cracked all over like crazy paving. The only time he was without his leather gilet was when he was sailing the Papa Westray; then he changed it for a much sea stained life jacket which was kept in the boat. He even wore the leather jacket when he drove Miss May round the island in the Reverend's battered old Ford. Going for a drive in the Ford was like being in a time warp. The doors opened the other way to normal and there were tiny orange indicators on each side of the car which flipped open with a large click to indicate left and right. When it was raining, Ivan would wind down the window and either hold out his arm straight or turn it in a circle getting his arm soaked in the process. Slowing down involved a measured flapping of the arm. Arvo, as he must now think of him, was a man of very few words. When you asked a question, he would never answer you directly but would look into the distance, puffing slowly on his pipe before answering with a monosyllable or as few words as he could get away with.

Catriona broke into the silence, saying 'I bet Arvo was a looker when he first came to the island. He kept a strong physique even into old age. I am surprised Dr MacCloud took him in with three daughters in the house, Miss May must have been quite young in the War.'

Finn said 'But Ivan lived in the old cottage in the kitchen garden, not in the house. Dr MacCloud no doubt felt that it was his duty to take in a prisoner of war. My father used to say that he would stand like a prophet of old in the pulpit and sternly declaim his sermons with that sing song intonation of the Highland preacher. Poor Ivan, hardly a barrel of laughs in that household. Have you been in the cottage?'

Jamie shook his head 'Not yet.'

The conversation moved on to the question of the trust which Miss May wanted to be set up to maintain the Manse. She had been quite specific in her will that she wanted the house to be made available for use by a young artist as rent free accommodation for up to six months at a time. There was a surprisingly large fund available to achieve this.

Jamie suggested that one possible way forward might be for Finn and Isla to move into the property, which could be remodelled internally to suit their family life, leaving them free to rent out the Watchman's cottage. Dr MacCloud's bedroom and study would be retained for the use of 'the young artist.' He had discussed this briefly with Catriona at the Manse and she had responded positively to the idea.

'We will have to take a look at the cottage. It might be possible to use it for the studio,' Jamie said.

These ideas sparked a lively debate during which a second bottle of wine was consumed without anyone particularly noticing. There was only one sharp moment when Catriona stuck one of her pointed shards into Jamie. She said 'Do you remember how Jamie used to go all "weird" as a child as if his thoughts were wading through a dense mist? How it used to spook us. Well, he still does "weird". When we were in the Boathouse and found the paintings, I lost him completely. It was like spending time with a sleep walker'.

Finn was sensitive to the barb in her comment. He quickly stepped in, saying 'I will never forget, Jamie, your prediction that Jonny Wilkinson would drop a goal in the dying moments of the Rugby World Cup final. I couldn't believe it when I watched the match live and it actually happened, just as you had predicted. Now what about this week's lottery numbers, Jamie?' They all laughed and the ice, which had briefly formed round Catriona's snide remark, melted away.

Rugged hills tumbled down to a wide arc of dunes bordering Garvaay Bay, where Lur Beag quietly nestled and waited. Jamie was walking back, full of good cheer after a lively evening with his friends. He did not need a torch, as the moon was white and fat with just an edge nibbled away. His path took him down through dunes topped with clumps of marram grass, which rustled eerily in the wind. The dunes looked silvery, almost ghostly, in the pale light of the moon. The duck boards, which his Grandfather had laid to prevent visitors from sinking into the sand, marked the way through the dunes. As Jamie crested the final dune he could see the cottage illuminated by the solar lights he had installed to light up the exterior of the cottage at night. He was glad to have the light to guide him the final way home.

His heart always missed a beat when he saw Lur Beag. It was a modernist gem, cleverly disguised to look vernacular to the island by the use of stones from two tumbled down cottages, once the homes of fishermen. The building was long and low as a nod to the island's ancient black houses. However, it broke from tradition by having a flat roof, which gave it a sharp, angular profile. His grandfather had had a large double glazed picture window ferried to the bay as there was no access via land. This was the western face of the cottage which gave onto an impressive view of their little bay and flooded the cottage with light. Otherwise, light was brought into the building by a series of tall narrow apertures like arrow slits penetrating a castle tower. The building chimed with Jamie's long held love of straight lines and symmetry. He could admire buildings with voluptuous curves like the Guggenheim in Bilbao but he was always drawn back to the sparing classical aesthetic.

The front door, which had been salvaged from one of the ruined cottages, was not locked (no one locked their doors on the island). He walked straight into a wooden vestibule, which greeted the visitor with an uplifting blast of scarlet on the walls. He flung his jacket on one of the simple ash pegs on the wall. He then entered the main room of the cottage. It was an open plan space, where the bedrooms and kitchen could be partitioned from the main living area by sliding Shoji walls consisting of opaque paper sheets on a lattice frame. The internal walls were panelled in a grained ply-wood which gave the spaces a warm, cocoon like feel, particularly the bedrooms. The floors were made of cork. There was also a minimalist Japanese aesthetic in terms of furnishing, especially in the bedrooms where mattresses lay on low wooden platforms in the centre of each room with tiny, wooden stools as bedside tables. Clothes were kept in willow baskets. The drama in the cottage came from large abstract paintings hung on the walls in which impasto white was slashed with wild black paint to create calligraphic shapes.

Jamie went into the kitchen for some water as he knew that he would feel dehydrated in the night after all the drinking. With the glass in his hand he went and sat down on the large sofa. The boxy walnut frame had been built in situ by a local cabinet maker to his grandfather's design, and, then upholstered in dark green, thick ribbed corduroy, which the sun had faded to an olive green. In front of the sofa was a smoked glass coffee table on which his grandfather had always kept a large pair of old fashioned binoculars. The sofa faced the large plate glass window through which there was a breathtaking view of Garvaay Bay; though much smaller than its neighbour, Bagh a Tomara, it was still stunningly beautiful. His grandfather would spend hours zooming in on the wheeling sea birds, the bobbing heads of grey seals and the humped back of a surfacing minke whale without ever moving from the sofa. Garvaay Bay had always felt like a private domain, tucked away from the other houses on the island, and steeped in history.

Jamie's gaze was inevitably drawn to the window but he could only see his own reflection in the glass. So he got up to turn off the spotlights which dotted the ceiling like stars. With the lights off he could see out of the window into the darkness. In the silver moonlight the familiar scene took on a metallic beauty. It was as if it had been etched out in sketchy white lines against a blue black background. He watched the distant breakers crash rhythmically onto the sand. The muffled murmur of the surf on the beach transformed the bay into an eerie and atmospheric place. He felt the urge to be out there in the wind and the sound of the sea, although it was well after midnight.

He plunged down the last dune which led directly onto the beach; his shoes rapidly filling with sand as he waded ankle deep in slithering sand. On the beach itself the sand was firm and he strode easily across it, drawn towards the hypnotic tide. He picked up a pebble and launched it high, watching it arch and then drop into the oncoming waves. The relentless march of the sea crashing towards him kept him a respectful distance from the water's edge. As he looked out to sea he could imagine on a moonlight night like this the rearing dragon prow of a Viking ship slipping stealthily towards the shore. A thousand years ago raiders, beguiled by the beauty of the island, had returned as settlers, their

Norse presence still locked down in the islanders' DNA.

His grandmother had told him that in the 1920s there had been a ferocious storm which had scoured the beach to reveal the fragments of three neolithic stone roundhouses. They had been excavated, photographed and then the sand was allowed to reclaim them, as the best way of preserving them. Polished stone mace heads, flint knives, and perfectly round stone balls, incised with mysterious concentric circles, had been discovered on the site and were now exhibited in the pre-history section of the National Museum of Scotland. On his many visits to the Museum as a child he had been thrilled to see these exhibits, which he regarded as his personal treasure coming, as they did, from his grandparents' beach. He could never walk this stretch of beach without feeling the deep pull of history.

The wind on his face had a sobering effect. He began to mull over in his mind the things they had been discussing that evening. He hoped that his suggestion that Finn and Isla be custodians of the Manse had not been crass. He knew that they were bursting at the seams in their tiny cottage with their three children and that money was tight. It seemed to him that they were the ideal candidates to manage the Manse. It was more than big enough to house their growing family, especially if they utilised the vast attic space. It would take him less than an hour to draw up suitable plans for an attic conversion. Finn and Isla would then be able to oversee the occupation of the first floor by a young artist in compliance with the terms of Miss May's will. It made sense to him but he worried that he had been clumsy in making the suggestion.

His thoughts then turned to Miss May herself. As his walk took him back and forth, parallel to the waves, it troubled him that the only figure missing from the nativity scene in the Boathouse was Miss May. Arvo had always been such a significant figure in her background, driving her around in the old Ford. One of the sisters must have given permission for Arvo to paint in the Boathouse. He instinctively felt that Miss May was the most likely sister. He had no real basis for thinking this other than she was, to him, the most artistically inclined of the three sisters. Thinking back to his childhood, he could conjure up the warm soundscape of her Chopin playing. He was conscious of his own romantic leanings and suspected that he was probably investing her with his own fantasies. Yet he could not explain to himself why, when he had looked at the watercolours in Dr Fergusson's cottage, it was the image of Miss May that had persisted in his mind. It was as if he could see her by the Boathouse window watching the sea dazzle and shimmer before her. He had never seen her painting. Nor had there been any sign of any paints in her bedroom or anywhere else in the Manse. Yet her image as an artist lingered. What else, he asked himself, could explain her explicit wish to help a young artist in her will?

The wind was keening across the bay, its screech drowning out the rhythmic sounds of the sea. It had a bitter, biting edge which was penetrating Jamie's jacket. His bones began to feel chilled. As he walked back to the cottage, he was still marvelling as to how Arvo and the mystery sister could have kept the painted chapel a secret for so long. It would still have been a secret had he and Catriona had not stumbled upon it. It was incredible to think that on all those occasions when he had been helping Arvo get the Papa Westray ready for sailing, the secret chapel had been silently waiting in the room above. The nativity scene was niggling away at him like a sore. It was a puzzle, which intrigued and frustrated him. He did not know why he felt this pressing need for some sort of resolution.

***

Jamie spent the next morning dealing with urgent emails and holding an internet meeting with his French assistant, Heloise, about the practice's latest project. The project was in its infancy and could be left for a short while but very soon it would need his full attention. Heloise, Ellie as he called her, was a bright and talented architect, but she worried unnecessarily when he was away for any length of time. Her insecurity stemmed from years of intellectual bullying by her domineering family. Her parents were academics in medical science and her older brothers were doctors in Paris. From a young age she had complained that all they ever talked about was medicine and the place reeked (metaphorically) of antiseptic. She proclaimed as loudly as she could that she was the artistic one and wanted nothing to do with medicine. This caused her endless friction and misery but finally her parents conceded. She enrolled for the architecture course at Edinburgh University and there met Jamie. He was immediately attracted by her mix of vulnerability and fierce courage. She still carried emotional bruises but, with his support, she had begun the long healing process. Seeing her on his computer screen had reminded him how much he missed her. She had been his assistant for five years, his girlfriend for three. She was stunning, tall, slender with rich chestnut hair tumbling down her back and the warmest of melting chocolate eyes. He would be a fool to leave her too long.

Jamie decided to skip lunch and visit Arvo's cottage. The kitchen garden was separated from the Manse and was surrounded by a medium height drystone wall as protection from the raw winds that frequently lashed the island. The garden was overgrown with the vegetables gone wild and native but you could still see its formal grid structure with raised wooden beds for the vegetables. Against the south facing wall old fruit trees had been planted with their gnarled branches spread eagled like ancient martyrs.

Nestled along the northern side of the wall was the gardener's cottage, a low stone building with a dark slate roof. Inside there was just one small room with a bathroom curtained off at one end. There was a wood stove in one corner, which still had an old iron kettle on it. As the fire had not been lit for some time, damp had been allowed to encroach. Mould mottled the once white washed walls with large green patches. The gardener at the Manse had always taken his meals in the kitchen of the house and so there was no cooker or fridge or dining table. There was a single bed along the wall with a trunk for clothes at its foot. A battered armchair with a faded tartan cushion hugged the stove. A large upturned plant pot served as a side table on which still rested Arvo's pipe and a box of Swan matches. There was a shelf near to the stove on which there was a white chipped tin mug, a Kilner jar with brown flakes at the bottom, where he kept his tobacco, and a tiny red transistor radio. They were all now covered in a layer of dust. The only other shelf was over the bed where there was a slate tile, broken at the edges, which had been simply propped against the wall. Jamie went over and took the slate down from the shelf. A crucifix had been carefully scratched into the surface, probably with nothing more elaborate than nail. Spartan, simple, hermetic. Nothing that could indicate a personality beyond an ascetic frugality. Jamie opened the trunk. Inside were a couple of denim shirts, a pair of brown corduroy trousers, some greying long Johns and an assortment of thick woollen socks. He was not sure what he was looking for, maybe a painter's smock or something which tied him to the Boathouse painter. There was nothing. Nevertheless Arvo had left a powerful presence in the cottage. He had died eighteen months before Miss May and it was obvious to Jamie that Miss May had deliberately left the cottage undisturbed.

Hanging behind the door was the long leather sleeveless jacket, which Jamie remembered so well. Jamie touched the jacket like a talisman as he was leaving the cottage. The feel and the smell of the old leather acted as a stimulant to his memory. The embryo of an idea was slowly surfacing into his consciousness. Suddenly he shouted out loud, angry with himself, 'Idiot! The Joseph in the Nativity painting must be a self portrait of Arvo himself. Although you can't see a face, he's dressed Joseph in his old leather coat. And he's identified himself as the painter by scratching the letters of his Christian name on the edge of Joseph's leather jerkin. It was staring us in the face all the time.' Jamie smiled. 'So there was a tiny part of this self effacing man that wanted recognition after all. I wonder...,' Jamie mused to himself, 'if Joseph was based on a real person, then maybe the Madonna and the baby were based upon real people too, but who?'

He pictured the Madonna's oval face. It was a mesmerising face, a classically sculpted, almond eyed Botticelli. There was again that flicker of recognition. Frustratingly it fizzled out as quickly as it had flared up in his memory. He really wanted to know. He needed to scratch the mental itch which was irritating him like the sharp nip of an island midge.

***

He found himself outside the imposing front door of the Manse. He had a half formed premonition that an answer was to be found somewhere in the Manse. He was not going to fight his intuition on this occasion. For once, he was going to cut his instincts loose, let them roam free roam through his mind until the fledgling idea was tracked down to its source.

He drifted into the drawing room, which was a handsome, restrained room, symmetrically proportioned, which he found so aesthetically pleasing. It was austerely furnished with two plain high backed settles facing one another, either side of an elegant but simple marble fireplace. Jamie could not imagine more uncomfortable seating, a disincentive to lingering on the part of the Reverend's visitors. The minimalism, nevertheless, appealed to his modernist principles. There was a stone flagged floor which, to his knowledge, had never been covered by a rug, even in winter. As the large sashed windows retained their original shutters, the windows were left bare. This meant that on sunny days the unencumbered sunlight streamed through the windows, stippling the flags with a warm, golden light.

His instincts were pulling him towards Miss May's piano which had been placed like an afterthought along the far wall. It was a 1930s upright grand with a rich mahogany case, which felt out of keeping with the otherwise spare effect of the room. It's presence was disturbing the symmetry of the room. Perhaps it was this jarring asymmetry which was drawing Jamie to it. He ran his hand across the keys which still sounded in tune. Just gently brushing the keys triggered a blast of muddled memories. He could see himself as a child dancing round and round, increasingly out of time with the rippling notes, until he fell dizzy to the ground.

'Get a grip' he said to himself, beginning to sense that this mental free fall was going to end badly. He knew he was slightly out of kilter like a drunken man about to lose his footing.

Feeling as if he was moving slowly underwater, he found himself lifting the hinged lid at the top of the case and peering into the workings of the piano. He saw the intricate fan shaped strings and neatly ordered wooden struts but nothing extraneous. He tried moving the piano a little way from the wall but it was too heavy. He got down on his knees and did his best to squint along the tiny gap between piano and wall. Other than dust there was nothing to be seen. He sat on the piano stool and tried to work out where this spool of irrationality was leading him but his mind would not settle. In this confused state, he stood up and lifted up the piano seat. He stared inside. As was to be expected, there were sheets of music. Jamie picked them up and shuffled through them. They were almost exclusively Miss May's beloved Chopin, nocturnes, preludes and mazurkas.

Part of his mind was saying 'What am I doing?' but he was in the grip now of this powerful intuition which was leading him onwards. He began tapping the sides and bottom of the inner compartment. The bottom rocked slightly. So he gave one side a mighty thwack with his fist. It raised up and he was able to prise away the bottom piece of wood to reveal a shallow cavity underneath.

He peered into the cavity. It contained an orange chiffon scarf. It was wrapped tightly round some object like the mummy of a small Egyptian cat. Jamie carefully unwound the scarf. A slim book and a photograph fell into his hand. The book had been beautifully tooled in dark orange Moroccan leather, which had worn round the edges. It was volume of poetry, 'Sonnets of Orpheus' by Rainer Maria Rilke. The book fell open at sonnet 15 and there was a mark against the first line of the second verse:

'Tanzt die orange. Wer kann sie vergessen...'

The photograph had been folded in the middle with the image invisible inside. He could tell that it was an old photograph because the paper was peppered with brown spots. It was torn in one corner. As it felt so fragile, he gingerly opened it up with shaking hands. It was the black and white image of a young man dressed in an SS uniform, gazing shyly at the camera lens. Jamie instantly knew who he was. With this shot of recognition, the fragments of the puzzle began to rearrange themselves and slot neatly into place in his head. The picture which had been hovering tantalisingly on the edge of his mind was now in focus. He felt relief but also fear. He had unleashed his inner genie and lost all control. He now wanted cohesion, weight, to moor him firmly to reality.

Jamie could only spend another day on the island. So he invited Catriona to a picnic on the Isle of the Standing Stone. This was not just a wallow in nostalgia. Over the last few days Catriona had made him sharply aware of her bitter sweet feelings towards him. There was a fissure in their friendship and he wanted to find a way of healing the breach.

He had checked that the motor of the Papa Westray was in working order. After a few tentative pulls, the engine coughed and stuttered into life. Catriona arrived with a tub of dark chocolate brownies. She was wearing a dark magenta dress and a calf length grey tweed jacket with the collar raised round her neck.

Catriona settled herself into the boat amongst the wicker picnic baskets. 'Looks like a proper feast' she said as she looked round the boat. Jamie laughed and then launched the Papa Westray down the Boathouse slipway with a strenuous heave. He leapt into the boat, inevitably getting his feet wet, and started the motor at the rear of the boat. The motor spluttered the usual engine expletives, as the Papa Westray began to plough a somewhat ungainly progress across the bay. The waves were unusually benign for a late summer day and slapped with a gentle, rhythmic lap against the wooden hull. The Papa Westray was styled on an old flat bottomed coastal boat called a Farthing. It had a distinctive terracotta sail, which flapped gloriously in the wind when the boat was on a reach. Jamie had hoped to sail the boat across the bay, but, as he struggled with the ropes and cleats, he realised that he had forgotten the knack of setting up the sail. So he had to rely on the outboard motor, which somewhat downgraded the spirit of adventure.

The boat left the shelter of the bay. It rocked and rolled alarmingly when it was first buffeted by the waves of the open sea but rallied and steadied and made good progress towards the island.

The island loomed before them. It was no more than an outcrop of rock but boasted on its summit a solitary prehistoric Standing Stone. Many were the legends as to how it had got there and what it was for. There was no denying that it was a spectacular monument to a forgotten time. Jamie had to steer the boat to the rear of the island where there was a crack in the rock through which a small boat could negotiate into a sheltered inlet. This gave onto a narrow shelf of sand, where Jamie beached the boat. They scrambled out and carried the baskets up a precipitous, zigzagging path to the top of the cliff.

As they breasted the lip of the cliff, a strong gust of wind slapped them in the face. It came suddenly roaring across the sea, driving away any fleeting impression of calm. Its ferocity took their breath away, as they bent into the wind and laboured their way towards the Standing Stone. The megalith stood like a finger pointing towards the sky, a sentinel from a bygone age. At the foot of the megalith to the right the rock had been hollowed out and provided a natural niche and shelter from the ravages of the sea borne wind. It was here that they laid out the tartan blanket and surrounded themselves with the hampers like a circle of wagons. They sat cross legged side by side on the blanket. From their vantage point they could look out onto the boiling seas beneath them and at the balletic seagulls swooping and wheeling in ever changing circles.

Jamie pulled out a bottle of champagne from one of the hampers. Having been bounced about in the boat, it erupted in a fountain of fizz as he popped the cork and sent showers of bubbly spray over both of them.

Laughing apologetically and mopping his face with a handkerchief, 'A toast to Miss May', he cried out so as to be heard over the wail of the wind. They both raised their champagne flutes and chanted together 'Miss May.'They then solemnly clinked their glasses in an unspoken celebration of the life which had mysteriously touched their own. Jamie produced from the hamper a beautifully poached wild salmon, cold new potatoes in a buttery chive sauce, a Greek style salad with green and black olives, red cherry tomatoes, chunks of cucumber and a scattering of rich feta cheese. The food was heaped onto large white china plates, which he had fished out of the second hamper. The second course followed the Miss May tradition: raspberries topped with double cream, which disappeared just as quickly as it had twenty years before.

Jamie took out from one of the baskets the orange chiffon scarf which he had re-wrapped round the book of poetry. He ceremoniously handed it to Catriona and, with a nod of his head, encouraged her to unravel the scarf. As she removed the scarf, she found the book and the photograph, both of which she examined intently. She looked enquiringly at Jamie.

He smiled and said 'I think I've cracked the enigma as to Arvo's helpmate...I found this book hidden in the piano stool of Miss May's piano. It was clearly of huge importance to her'.

Catriona said 'But it's in German?'

Jamie said 'It's a book of Rilke's poems. Go to the tagged page, do you see the pencil marks alongside the words of the second verse "Tanzt die Orange. Wer kann sie vergessen"'.

Catriona said 'What does that mean?'

Jamie said 'I think it translates as "Dance the orange. Who can forget it..." Think back to the picnic on this spot when we were ten years old, the picnic where I proposed to you beneath the Standing Stone. Miss May must have overheard us because I recall her laughing at us in a teasing way but then she became quite intense, saying over and over again"Always dance the orange"'.

Catriona looked baffled 'I remember your proposal but nothing else?'

Jamie said patiently 'OK, this is my theory. I believe that this is a photograph of Arvo, when he was a young soldier in the German army. Look at the uniform...it's the uniform of the Waffen-SS. The only soldier in a German uniform whom Miss May could have known was Arvo. He must have given his photograph to her and, I like to think, the Rilke poems as well. Both book and photograph were of great sentimental value to her because she kept them hidden in a place which was special only to her, her beloved piano.' He hesitated for a moment before he took a reckless punt on Catriona's reaction. The odds were that she would think him mad.

'I have this powerful notion, this feeling that they loved one another. These Rilke poems were his gift to her as a token of their unspoken love. In return, her gift to him was the opportunity to use his remarkable talents to create the chapel, a sort of visual hymn to his Estonian past, to the kindness of the people of his adopted home and to his secret feelings for Miss May. I am pretty sure she was with him when he worked on the murals and painted her own watercolours looking out of the Boathouse window onto the Bay. Of course, I could be completely wrong...inventing a wild fantasy of my own...'

He was expecting a sharp, cynical response but Catriona sat in silence, surprisingly thoughtful about what he had said. He looked out towards the sinuous undulations of the sea, its foam topped waves breaking on the rocks of the island below. He did not want to interrupt her thoughts.

Eventually she said, almost sadly. 'The chapel does cast a spell upon you. That large orange moon. It's hypnotic and draws you into its surreal world. ' She turned to him and looked at him directly 'It's mad but I actually believe you. Do you think they made love there in the chapel?'

Jamie shook his head 'No, I don't think so. It was more of a spiritual love. If you like, a coupling of two artistic souls rather than anything sexual. Miss May was surely too much a daughter of the Manse but it's my guess that there was regret that they found themselves unable to break down the barriers of convention.

'Why do you say that?'

'Rilke's Sonnets are poems of love but also of infinite regret; Orpheus losing his Eurydice as she is brought back to the very threshold of the living world. I believe that Miss May understood the pain of regret. I think she saw us as childhood sweethearts. That's why she wanted us to 'dance the orange,' to keep the joy of our childhood love alive.'

'My God, do you think that's why she chose us as her executors, like match making beyond the grave. I guess she must have seen us as the inheritors of her own dreams,' said Catriona. Then she laughed bitterly, 'Well, that piece of wishful thinking went spectacularly wrong, didn't it!'

'Why do you say that?' remonstrated Jamie 'As far as I am concerned, you are a very special person in my life and always will be.'

He could not help himself from adding 'But for years now, it's been you who hasn't let me into your life. What did I do that was so wrong?'

'You still don't get it, do you? I wanted more than your friendship, more than just a bit part in your childhood memories. I wanted feelings, emotion, love but I was Miss Invisibility to you and it hurt.' This burst out like an angry explosion of emotion, long pent up, and then she struggled to hold back the tears 'Jamie McHugh, as distant as ever. God, it still hurts after all this time.'

Jamie's mouth went very dry. 'I am sorry', was all he could think to say.

'I don't want you to be sorry' she spat at him, her eyes blazing through the glitter of tears.

He fell silent and bowed his head like a penitent. Her words ached like bruises.

'I know I am being ridiculous. I am married, for God's sake, but these last few days together have been a mistake, stoked up bad feelings for me from the past. I love Paul, I really do,' she began to weep, 'But that's gone wrong too like everything in my life.'

He instinctively put his arm round her shaking shoulders. She flinched but then relaxed against him. She tried to smile though her tears.

'I am sorry. It's my hormones running riot. I'm an emotional mess right now...I want a child, Jamie. My biological clock is in overdrive but Paul just won't listen to me. It has become an obsession that goes round inside my head. I can't control it and it's driving me mad. I will do anything to have a child.'

She shuddered as if suddenly chilled.

'I can't blame Paul because if I do it's the end of our marriage. I don't want that because until now it's been a good...a brilliant marriage. Paul has been a kind, loving, thoughtful husband, always there for me when I need him. He's a gifted surgeon, committed to his patients. Yet he always finds quality time for me, which he fills with fun and laughter. When we first married, we talked and talked about starting a family. It was something we both longed for...so I can't understand why he's suddenly so obdurate that he doesn't want a child. He's never been thoughtless to me before. This change of heart is so out of character that I have begun to wonder if he is ill. But he won't discuss it with me...just shuts up like a clam. It's bewildering. Our relationship has been so magical and, I guess, I don't want the magic to stop. I feel this gnawing sense of loss and I can't bear it...So Jamie, please be my scapegoat. Just for a short time, let me heap the blame for my current misery on you...for what might have been between us. I am sorry, I am not making any sense.'

Jamie hugged her tightly 'No, it makes sense. If I am ever a bastard again, just tell me straight'.

Catriona gave her tears a harsh wipe and, shaking him off, climbed out of their niche to stand in the shadow of the Standing Stone. It was a massive piece of grey blue stone, shaped like the blade of a leaf, at least nine foot high and an arm span thick, patched with mustard yellow lichen. Jamie joined her and ran his hand across the ridged markings. By touching the texture of the stone he was for a moment lost in the mystery of the extraordinary people who had hewn this giant lump of granite with nothing more than stone axes and had somehow transported the stone to this little outcrop of rock. He was profoundly moved by a sense of timelessness.

The late summer night was drawing in and the changeable wind had dropped to a murmur. The deep blue sky was blushing faint blotches of pink. Catriona was drawn to the front of the megalith, still warm in the rays of the dying sun. She pulled Jamie close to her. They leant side by side against the Stone. Catriona sighed deeply, and, as if reading his earlier thoughts, she murmured 'Infinity' and then very softly 'Infinity of regret'. Her hand sought out Jamie's hand. He gripped it, a gesture of solidarity and, he hoped, of reconciliation.

The megalith was growing cold but they lingered a few moments more, silhouetted together against the Stone, facing an engorged sun which had turned a spectacular blood orange against the inky violet of the darkening sky.

***

Jamie steered the Papa Westray towards the slipway of the Boathouse. It was a tricky manoeuvre and the boat grounded on a ridge of sand just short of the slipway. There was nothing for it but to get out of the boat into the freezing water to haul the boat onto the slipway. As Jamie was manhandling the boat inside the Boathouse, Catriona grabbed the picnic rug out of it and started drying her feet with it.

'This is way too cold', she said. There was a short pause before she added as if on impulse, 'Let's go and look at the chapel again'.

'It'll be dark up there'.

'I've got matches. There are loads of candles up there. Come on, don't you want to see the chapel illuminated in candle light.'

Without waiting for an answer, she disappeared into the gloom of the Boathouse, while Jamie pulled the protective tarpaulin cover over the boat. As he finished, he could hear Catriona shouting 'Come on Jamie. This is awesome'. He could see a glow in the hatchway which gave access to the chapel. It lighted his way to the ladder.

As he emerged into the chapel, he was instantly entranced by the ethereal beauty of the space with the ravishingly beautiful frescoes highlighted in the flickering light of the candles. He turned in a slow circle drinking in the eerie, introspective atmosphere of swirling forests and supernatural lakes, all bathed in the rich smell of frankincense from the burning candles. The candle light added shadows which gave an uncanny quality of depth, haunting pools of darkness, to the paintings.

Catriona was fiddling with the tape recorder 'I've got some new batteries for the tape recorder and if they work, we will find out what Arvo was listening to' she said. She then cried out triumphantly 'Yes, they fit' and held out the tape recorder to Jamie, 'Come on, Jamie, do the honours!'

Jamie went over to her and, smiling, pressed the top button on the machine. There was no sound for a moment and then a faint whirring noise, as if the machine was cranking itself into life. Suddenly, the room was filled with the deep sonorous chanting of the Russian Orthodox liturgy. The music growled from the very depths of the soul, swelling into mighty crescendo of raw, spiritual emotion before dying down to an echoing murmur. With each crescendo Jamie felt he was surfacing from a dark, bottomless ocean into the glittering, light of the moon. Bathed in the glorious resonant sound, he stood in front of the nativity scene. There was the kneeling Joseph, who he now clearly saw as a self portrait of Arvo. He then looked into the eyes of the Madonna and the kindly eyes of a much younger Miss May looked back at him. He felt a deep sense of peace wash over him. He had finally retrieved her identity from the loose fragments floating at the back of his mind.

Catriona stood beside him, staring at the figure of Mary. She said more to herself than to Jamie 'Who is it?'

Jamie whispered 'It's a portrait of Miss May. Look long and hard into those almond eyes. We only knew Miss May when she was old, her eyes dimmed with age. This sparkle is how she must have looked when Arvo first saw her in the last years of the War, when she was young, lithe and vibrant. He kept that youthful image locked in his head until he could release it into paint'.

'It is good that they are together. The baby?' she asked Jamie.

'I think that the painting is an act of faith and so the baby is a religious icon, a symbol of piety, which they both deeply felt. Perhaps, subliminally the baby was also a symbol of their unspoken love. I like to think so, but I'm just guessing...'

He turned to Catriona. He saw that she had tied her hair back with the orange chiffon scarf, which freaked him momentarily. Catriona turned to face him. Impulsively she kissed him full on the mouth. A dark crimson flush was transfiguring her face almost beyond recognition. Before he could process what was happening, she had pulled his face towards her and began to kiss him again full on the lips. She pushed him back against the mural, trying to possess him with her green cat eyes. He could feel the heat radiating out from her body and found himself capitulating to the irresistible erotic rhythm pulsating through her. She began tearing urgently at his clothing and he could not help himself from responding. Together they lost all sense of themselves until they reached a mutual climax. For her, it was an affirmation of life in the face of overwhelming grief. For him, it was a consoling, healing sort of love. Breathless and spent, they slid down the wall together and sat with their backs to the mural of the nativity. They started laughing hysterically in disbelief as to what had just happened.

Suddenly Jamie heard a 'halloo' coming from the bottom of the ladder. He tried to pull up Catriona who was still helpless with laughter. Her legs kept collapsing under her like the rubbery legs of newly born foal. Suddenly sober, Jamie physically manhandled her upright. He was still vigorously brushing down her dress, as Finn's head bobbed up though the hatchway. As he looked round the chapel, he gasped 'Wow! This is amazing'. He clambered into the chapel and began to wander round the chapel, looking at the murals in an excited state of awe. He could not help exclaiming 'wow' every second or so. Jamie and Catriona did not move. The shock of reality had hit them like a cold shower and had extinguished their brief, heady elation. Jamie felt a sense of shame. Icy fingers of foreboding were stealing up his spine. They had desecrated a spiritual place and cast a dark shadow over the Nativity. Something black had entered their lives.

In his circumnavigation of the chapel, Finn had reached the nativity scene, which Jamie and Catriona were still partly blocking. Finn was no longer gazing at the paintings but was looking at them, a surprised expression crossing his face. He began to take in their dishevelled appearance and the strange silence. He stared from one to the other. After a moment or two, he swallowed hard as if there was a lump which he had to clear in his throat. 'Wow' he said very quietly to himself, 'I think I had better go.' He turned on his heel and disappeared quickly down the ladder.

## Part Two

After a quick shower Jamie dressed quietly. Ellie was still sleeping curled up beneath the duvet. He loved this time of the morning when he opened up his house to the sunlight. He felt like a magician opening the secret drawers of his box of tricks. He began to descend the staircase from the bedroom landing alongside the book shelves which lined the whole of the wall. They were painted a pillar box red and filled with large format art and architecture books. Above the shelves there was a run of small windows, each with its own shutter system used to harness heat and light. Arming himself with a hooked pole, he stepped onto the sliding steel ladder, which gave him access to the books. Sliding easily across the book case, he expertly manipulated the pole so as to catch the hooks on the shutters and pull each shutter down allowing the early morning light to flood the stairwell. In the hallway he moved a louvred shutter to allow light to filter through the glass blocks beside the front door.

He slipped out of the front door and walked up Old Hailes Row, turning left onto Dunkeld Street and then right onto Gladstone Street. Two shops along Gladstone Street there was a newsagent shop which opened early and sold freshly baked croissant along with newspapers and magazines. He nodded a greeting to the young Asian girl behind the till, as he did every morning, and bought a range of newspapers and two almond croissant, which she wrapped up in a brown paper bag for him. The air was fresh as he walked briskly back.

Old Hailes Row was cobbled and sloped steeply away from Dunkeld Street. It was on the eastern end of the

New Town. The house sat in a space between the rear of the two storey Georgian houses on Dunkeld Street and the gable end of the Old Hailes Row houses, which stepped down the street with staggered facades. It had been an ugly derelict gap, which the City planners had been happy to see developed in an innovative way.

The footprint measured just twelve metres by seven metres, into which he shoehorned a building tiered like one side of a ziggurat which was faced with stone to mimic the surrounding Georgian houses. The exterior was geometric, austere, monumental and elegant. It had the same pared down style and economy of interior space as its older Georgian neighbours.

With considerable ingenuity, he had managed to fit within the main central tier an open plan living, dining, kitchen area arranged on different levels. The kitchen was raised like an altar so that he could cook and still communicate with friends in the living space. The living space opened out into a tiny roof courtyard, the walls painted terracotta and broken up with green trellis panels, over which honeysuckle and white flowering jasmine were beginning to climb. The floor of the courtyard was tiled in a striking pattern of black and terracotta tiles. Tubs of bay trees added to the sense of a sun warmed Mediterranean terrace in stark contrast to the towering grey stone walls of the surrounding properties.

The main bedroom took over the whole of the next tier. The top tier housed two smaller bedrooms with shower rooms, which nestled under a glazed sloping roof where the light was regulated by a motorised shutter. With the shutter open it felt like sleeping under the stars. Into the basement he fitted flexible multi purpose rooms, one of which served as a study and guest bedroom and the other was both a shower and laundry room. He had used mirrors to play tricks with the natural light and create illusions of space. At the foot of the main staircase there was a full length, slightly foxed mirror which deceived the eye into believing that it was an extension of the corridor.

Holding the bag of croissants and newspapers close to his chest with one hand, he juggled the key in the lock with the other and pushed the door open with his knee. Immediately opposite the front door in the hallway was a floor to ceiling black and white abstract painting which Jamie had commissioned from his old school friend, Freddie Gough, to remind him of his grandparents' paintings in the cottage. It was a striking image on entering the house. Jamie stopped a moment in front of the painting, which he always did, before running up the stairs to the kitchen. The kitchen was compact and fastidiously organised to maximise the space, the cupboards regimented with labelled glass containers containing rice, pasta, pulses and spices. With one practised movement he switched on the kettle, reached for two large earthen ware mugs and two plates, scooped coffee into the percolator and placed the still warm croissant on the plates.

Three minutes later he climbed up the stairs with a tray on which the mugs of steaming coffee were carefully balanced with the newspapers tucked under his arm. His clattering up the wooden stairs had caused Ellie to stir beneath the duvet. He loved watching her unfurl like a cat, turn on her back with a yawn and then throw her arms wide to embrace wakefulness. 'Coffee,' he announced unnecessarily and then kissed her. It was part of their morning ritual. Her response was to shuffle up the bed and prop herself against the pillows. Jamie handed her one of the mugs, placed the tray on the end of the bed and joined her. She sank back into the pillows and caressed her mug of coffee whilst he rifled through the papers and nibbled at a croissant. She suddenly jolted and said 'The baby is kicking hard. He's...she's a footballer'. Jamie placed his hand on her stomach and felt the faint flickers of movement. They both laughed.

The ringtone of a mobile phone in a distant room suddenly broke through their contentment. As he shifted, 'Oh, leave it' Ellie said lazily, 'Whoever it is will leave a message or ring again'. He settled back against the pillows and drank deeply from his mug of coffee, relishing their shared moment together.

Twenty minutes later he picked up the mobile phone as he was about to leave for work. He had left it on top of a pile of books on the glass coffee table in the living room. He saw that there was a recorded message and pressed play. The voice was hesitant and thick but he recognised the gentle Highland cadences of Finn.

Finn was apologising for leaving a message on the phone, saying it was not right to leave a message but he could not wait as Jamie needed to know. The voice cracked at this point, followed by a brief pause, as if Finn was swallowing hard. With an obvious struggle he went on 'It's bad, Jamie. There is no easy way of telling you.' He paused again before continuing, 'Catriona is dead, Jamie. Killed in a car crash. Her husband has been flown to Glasgow and is in intensive care. Her little boy is here with his Grandad. He was thrown from the car and is mercifully unharmed. Catriona's father is distraught and is saying that you must come and see him. At times he loses it, totally loses it, which is so uncharacteristic that it frightens us all. Jamie, you must come. It's bad, very bad. His son is arranging the funeral, probably for this Sunday. I know time is short but her father needs it to be...so that he can begin to.... I don't know what to say. It's just bad. I am so sorry to tell you like this'. Finn's voice broke down completely and the message abruptly ended.

Jamie stood stock still, all life leaching out of his body, leaving him arid and spent. The denial 'It can't be true' was screaming round and round in his head but the deadened beat of his heart and the nausea welling in the pit of his stomach were telling him otherwise. 'Ellie, Ellie,' he shouted hoarsely.

Alarmed at the distress in his voice, she came running down the stairs, her dressing gown slipping down her shoulders, her feet bare.

'What is it, Jamie? What on earth is it?' she said as she entered the living room and saw him frozen in the centre of the room. She rushed to him and, putting her arms round him, repeated 'What is it?'

He turned to her and buried his head in her arms.

'Please Jamie. What's wrong?' she implored.

Lifting his head, he whispered 'Catriona is dead'.

Ellie sank down slowly onto the sofa, as the shock absorbed her. He sat down beside her and, with his head in his hands, mumbled in broken phrases 'She was killed... In a car crash...Her son is alive...It was Finn on the phone... The funeral is on Sunday'. He then said 'I will have to go'.

She put her hand on his shoulder and said quietly 'Of course' but then turned away to look through the large glass windows onto the terrace where the sun was casting shadows onto the terracotta wall. She was trying to suppress the well of jealousy which rose like gorge at the mention of Catriona's name. It was wholly inappropriate, she knew, but she could not help it.

***

Finn was waiting for him in the arrival area of the island airport, which was no more than a landing strip amidst close cropped grass. They hugged one another for a long time but said nothing. Finn merely picked up Jamie's overnight case and carried it to his battered old jeep parked on the grass. Jamie's cottage had been let for the summer and so he was staying for the funeral at Tarkavay House, where Finn's family had relocated. Jamie was relieved, as he did not want to be on his own to confront his memories. He had been spooked by Catriona's death. Foreboding had been festering within him like an infected wound for a long time. There was a sense of guilt too, though he could not explain why. He was ashamed that he felt like this. He kept telling himself that it was merely the shock of her dying so young, but deep down he was not sure what was driving his feelings.

They drove in silence. Slanting rain from a forbidding sky lashed a persistent stream of water against the windscreen, the frantic windscreen wipers giving only feeble resistance. The windows rapidly steamed up creating a fog which cut them off from the outside. As quickly as Finn rubbed a clear patch on the windscreen, the steam was already reforming. The atmosphere within the car was heavy and claustrophobic.

After struggling for a time, Finn said 'I am sorry. I am going to have to open the windows to get rid of this steam'. The front passenger windows slid down and the rain hissed and spat on Jamie's face as he turned to look out of the window. The journey across the island was rooted in him like a mind map. For years, whenever he found sleep difficult, he would trace every twist and turn of the journey in his mind's eye. He rarely finished the memory journey before succumbing to waves of sleep.

The single track shone like a glistening ribbon in the rain. It undulated across moorland, which was woven in the colours of amber and magenta and punctuated by bronze coloured lochans. It rose through the stunted and twisted trees of an ancient birch wood, long strands of lichen dripping from gnarled branches. It ran alongside a loch of shimmering, rippling silver, fringed by the delicate green spear heads of reeds. Finally it cut through the rocky outcrop which bordered the bay and plunged down towards the shore with its spectacular view of the Torrenish peaks looming across the bay.

Before the track wound its way through the rocks, there was a passing place into which Finn suddenly steered the jeep. The vehicle stopped dead with a bump. He sat still for a moment, staring straight ahead. Jamie looked at him enquiringly. Finn shook his head and said grimly 'That's where the accident happened'.

This stark statement jolted Jamie out of his reverie. He instantly got out of the car and walked towards a jutting outcrop, which had caused the track to skirt around it to the right. The unremitting rain was already soaking him through to the skin but he was sharply focused and did not notice. At the foot of the rock were several poignant bouquets of flowers, ragged and limp in the rain. He bent down to read their hand written messages but the rain had drained them of all legibility. These were the only tell tale signs that a fatality had occurred. All the debris from the crash had been removed. There were no skid marks gouged on the track to bear witness to what, he imagined, must have been the desperate braking of the car. Only if you looked carefully at the rock, could you see that there was a gash, where the left hand side of the car had been embedded. It was fresh and raw, the exposed underlying rock gleaming lighter in the rain.

Finn had joined Jamie and they stood side by side in the rain. Rain drops ran down their faces and discreetly masked their own grief. Finn broke their silence by clearing his throat and observing bleakly 'He must have been driving at a hell of a speed'.

'An insane speed' murmured Jamie as he looked at the rock and then back down the road. A half image flashed in his mind's eye for a second, a glimpse of a car careering wildly. It was accelerating towards the rock, not braking. He heard a woman's screams. The image then broke and distorted like in a shattered mirror. An involuntary shudder ran through him as if someone was walking over his grave. It was a deeply unpleasant feeling which left a bitter after taste.

***

It was a steep climb up to the kirk, which clung to a rocky promontory overlooking the bay. Its thick stone walls were constantly under attack from the westerly wind, which raked the waters of the bay into white topped, angry waves. Half buried tombstones, listing at strange angles, were scattered on either side of the path and added to the sense of desolation.

Jamie joined the straggling group of local mourners who were proceeding with slow solemnity up the precipitous path. The women were clinging on to their hats in the face of the howling gale.

‘Mercifully it’s not raining’, Jamie thought to himself. A pale sun was indeed trying to break through the heavy canopy of cloud.

As he got closer to the knot of people standing outside the kirk porch, Jamie wished that he had some task to distract himself from the morbid thoughts swirling around in his mind. Isla was singing during the service and Finn was accompanying her on the pipes. For a brief moment he felt envious. Then he remembered how they had both expressed their nervousness at performing on such an emotional occasion. He shook his head. Maybe it was as well that he was merely a spectator. He was prone to get emotional and he was so overwrought today he could easily break down. He knew full well that any emotional display would be met with the disapproving grimaces of the stiff lipped islanders and the last thing he wanted to do was to embarrass Catriona’s father.

It had been due to the efforts of Catriona’s father that the kirk, which had fallen into disuse after the death of the Reverend MacCloud, had recently been reconsecrated. A Minister from one of the larger islands was now flown in to officiate on special occasions such as island weddings and funerals. Catriona’s father could never have imagined that his daughter would be one of the first to be buried after the reconsecration.

Jamie was glad when he finally reached the tiny church porch, as it at least provided some protection from the wind. He was immediately ushered into the kirk itself by the stooping figure of Finlay Martin, the sessions clerk, who was busily greeting mourners at the door. As he stepped inside Jamie was immediately struck by the amount of light which filled the kirk through the clear glass widows high up in the walls.

There were only five plain wooden pews on each side of a narrow aisle and he saw with dismay that they were already filling up. He decided to remain standing in the small space at the back of the pews. It would have seemed wrong to try and push his way into a crowded pew, especially as everyone was being very quiet as befitted the occasion.

Having settled in his position, he had a moment to look round the kirk, which he had not been in since he was a child. He could see Finn and Isla at the front of the kirk. Then he saw the simple wooden coffin and Catriona's father with his head bowed, resting both hands on the coffin lid. He audibly gasped, causing the occupants of the rearmost pew to turn round and look pointedly at him.

A nauseous wave of grief overwhelmed him. He suddenly felt unsteady as if he was on the deck of tiny boat on a tossing sea. He had to grip the back of the pew; otherwise he would have fallen. As he was desperately trying to recover himself, the door was shut behind him and the Minister, newly arrived from the airstrip, began to welcome the congregation to the solemn occasion.

As the service proceeded, Jamie marvelled at the stoicism of the mourners, in particular Catriona's father who stood like granite with his son, Euan, and young grandson, Joe, at his side. The hymns were sung with strong, resolute voices save for Jamie. He had choked at the first one and thereafter merely mouthed the words. In order to get through the service without breaking down, he tried to concentrate on the clouds which he could see out of the windows. It was too painful to look at the coffin. Part of him still could not believe that his friend was lying lifeless inside. Unwelcome images of his love making in the Boathouse began to intrude. He screwed his eyes shut to banish the images. They felt mortifying and shameful within sight of Catriona's coffin and her father's bowed head. Isla's soaring voice in a traditional lament, accompanied by the raw strains of Finn's bagpipe, penetrated the fog of his misery. Jamie wanted to howl and, overcome with a sickening claustrophobia, he abruptly turned, pushed his way to the door and walked out of the kirk.

As so often happened in the Highlands, in the short space of time that Jamie had been inside the kirk, the gale force wind had suddenly dropped. The sun had finally pierced through the blanket of clouds, which no longer had the monopoly of the sky. Ragged patches of blue signalled a kinder turn in the weather. It was amazing how merely a glint of sunshine transformed an otherwise bleak scene. Jamie stood with his back to the kirk door and took deep breaths to calm himself down. After a moment or two he began to walk among the gravestones, trying to make out the names of the long dead hidden under the lichen. Sheep, specks of white and black against the dun coloured hillside, bleated in the distance. It struck him how the past haunted this landscape. He could see the tumbled down stone walls of crofts, long since abandoned. He could see the ridges that scarified the pasture, a sign of the old system of heaping up rows of seaweed to fertilise the poor quality soil. These ridges were only visible in strong sunlight. He then squinted out towards the glinting sea and watched the waves forming long undulating lines. For a few seconds they reared up like giant horsemen but then broke ranks in a ragged whirl of white foam. The endless repetitive crash of the waves brought him a superficial sense of peace but, beneath it, lingered a painful recognition that something very precious had gone.

He felt an overmastering urge to visit the Boathouse again. He knew it was folly but maybe looking at Arvo's mural would bring about some form of catharsis. He followed the serpentine road down to the shore. The tide was high and so he kept to the road. A spray as fine as mist drifted on the air and he could taste the salt on his lips. The screeching of the long tailed terns was intense as they criss-crossed the waves with flashes of white and black, the swallows of the sea.

As he approached the Boathouse he could see that it had been repainted a Scandinavian style dark red and that new windows panes were being painted white. Finn had mentioned to him that the community was hoping to make Arvo's murals a tourist attraction rather like the Italian Chapel on Orkney in order to boost the economy of the island. Finn was currently engaged in converting the ground floor into a small cafe, which would sell coffee and home baked cakes to the hoped for tourists. The side door had been propped open by a large tin of white paint. He stepped cautiously inside. The sepulchral dark of its previous incarnation as a boat house had been replaced by a bright interior, the sun streaming through the brand new windows. In place of the double doors at the front of the Boathouse, there was now a large plate glass window through which Jamie had a dazzling view of the full sweep of Bagh a Tomara. As it was high tide, waves were slapping against the window. At the other end of the Boathouse was the half built carcass of a counter, which Finn was building for the cafe. He had also built a robust wooden slatted staircase up to Arvo's chapel.

Jamie slowly climbed the staircase. His breathing had become very rapid, as if he was running at full pelt, and his heart was beating unpleasantly in his chest, almost choking him. As he entered into the Chapel, he was captivated again by the shimmering forests, painted so realistically that it felt as if he was emerging amongst the swaying birch trees. The mesmerising swirls of the waxing orange moon captured his gaze. It seemed as if the moon was rotating wildly and drawing him into its vortex. He had to drag his eyes away to stop himself from being swallowed whole by its the yawning mouth. Before he had barely regained his balance, he was again overwhelmed, this time by the overpowering figure of the Madonna. He could not breathe and had to sit down on the bench, which was still there. He held his head in his hands until his heart beats began to slow down. He knew now that it had been a mistake to come there on the day of Catriona's funeral. There was to be no redemption, just an irrational sense of foreboding and the empty feeling of survivor guilt. He looked up in despair at the child figure of Catriona, so young, so full of life, and noticed for the first time a flash of vivid colour just to the left of her sandal. He stood up and peered closely at the mural. It was a delicately painted, large orange moth. Was Catriona about to crush it with her foot? Fear insinuated itself into his mind and he could feel the weight of darkness.

***

As the sun was dropping heavy and red onto the misty horizon Jamie made his way to Dr Fergusson's cottage. Catriona's father had been insistent that he wanted to see Jamie on his own after the funeral. It seemed that everybody on the island had felt it their duty to give Jamie this message during the course of the day. He was at a loss as to why he had been specifically summoned. Finn who had been the principal messenger had been tight lipped and had told him nothing, which added to Jamie's sense of unease.

Full of trepidation like a nervous schoolboy at the door of the headmaster's study, Jamie knocked hesitantly and heard 'Come on in. It's open' from inside the cottage. As he walked into the hallway, he saw in the doorway to the kitchen a small figure of a boy with long, light auburn hair He was wearing a large apron which was too big for him and had bunched round his waist where the apron strings had been wound round and round. A pair of red Wellington boots peeped out from underneath the apron. He was holding up to his mouth a huge chocolate cookie, as he turned back to stare at Jamie over his shoulder. There was something about the child that struck a chord with Jamie but he only managed to say 'Hi there' before the boy ran back into the kitchen. He realised that it was Catriona's son, Joe, who he had seen with his grandfather at the kirk. He remembered thinking at the time that surely he was too young to attend a funeral.

He heard another 'Come on in' command issuing, somewhat more impatiently, from the sitting room and, without another thought, he hastened into the room.

Dr Fergusson was sitting in his worn armchair with a decanter of whisky and two glasses on a little wooden table to his left. He motioned Jamie to sit down on the armchair opposite him and immediately began pouring the whisky into the glasses.

'You've seen my grandson, Joe', he said and tried to give Jamie a smile, which was painful to see.

Jamie nodded and mumbled his condolences for the second time that day as he stretched out to take the proffered glass. Dr Fergusson leaned back. He usually radiated an avuncular warmth which shed a glow on all those in his presence but tonight a chill was emanating from him like a dank winter fog. His eyes were cold, the steely blue of a mackerel's back. The cold went through Jamie. He was ashamed that he felt so uncomfortable with a man he had known all his life. However much his grief was hurting him, it was unimaginably worse for Catriona's father.

Dr Fergusson stared deeply into the depths of his glass, as if it held some arcane mystery, and, without looking at Jamie, said very quietly 'Paul killed her'.

Jamie swallowed hard and said 'I'm sorry?'

Dr Fergusson repeated more loudly 'Paul killed Catriona'.

Jamie shuffled unhappily in his chair at the emphatic word 'kill'. He felt instantly as he had when, as a child, he had been thrown into the deep end of a swimming pool and had floundered hopelessly out of his depth. In attempt to steer the conversation away from treacherous waters, he murmured 'A terrible, terrible accident'.

Dr Fergusson spoke with greater stress, his lips tightening with tension. 'It was no accident.'

Jamie saw again, like a flashback, the image of a car accelerating towards a rock. He closed his eyes to rid himself of the image which had seared his mind. He tried to stay calm but without success.

After a slight pause, Dr Fergusson added 'He was trying to kill the whole family.'

It was a plain statement of fact. The rational part of Jamie's mind baulked at what Dr Fergusson was saying. The irrational part of his mind, bedevilled by his own demons since viewing the crash site, rendered him incapable to offering any resistance. He felt as if he had been hooked with a barb like a fish and that Dr Fergusson was reeling him in ever closer to an unpleasant place, where he knew instinctively that he did not want to go.

Dr Fergusson reached down for a large brown envelope which had been resting against the legs of the side table. He withdrew from the envelope an assortment of photographs which he handed to Jamie, saying 'Have a look through these.'

Jamie's mind was racing as to where he was being taken. But wherever it was, he knew he was not going to like it. He nevertheless shuffled through the photographs. They were old black and white photographs of his three childhood friends and himself. They had been taken either in the garden of Dr Fergusson's cottage or on the beach in front of it.

'Am I looking for something in particular?' Jamie asked.

'Does anything strike you?'

Jamie felt a spark of anger 'No, I am sorry it doesn't. I don't like playing this sort of cat and mouse game.' He tried to hand back the photographs. He found himself on the defensive and his temples were beginning to throb.

'Humour me for a little longer' was the reply, as Dr Fergusson took the photographs from him, rifled through them and then selected one in particular which he handed back to him. It showed Jamie aged about four or five with his long hair well below his collar. He had his back to the camera but was looking over his shoulder at the photographer. He had a quizzical look on his face. This was the only photograph that showed his face in close up; the others were more distant images. Jamie stared at the photograph. He had seen this image recently but for the life of him could not remember where.

'Perhaps I am being unfair,' Dr Fergusson said with a gentler tone to his Highland burr, 'Maybe you've not had long enough'.

'I am completely baffled, I am afraid' said Jamie.

'Let me tell you a story' said Dr Fergusson, at which Jamie almost audibly groaned. 'Am I being punished for something?' he asked himself. He felt he was being taunted and became aware that he was clenching and unclenching his hands. As he had always looked up to Dr Fergusson, he was mortified that he had appeared to have lost his respect.

'I've asked you to humour me' Dr Fergusson said sharply and Jamie held up his hand in submission. He told himself that grief can make even the gentlest of men granite faced, even cruel.

'There was an unhappy young woman who married for love. The husband, bright, gifted, caring, was the ideal man for this prickly young woman and, by his devotion, he found a way of making her happy. They both deeply wanted a child together. Then overnight the husband changed. He said that he no longer wanted a child.' Jamie jolted as if electrocuted by a nasty shock. 'This killed their love. The desire for a child dominated every waking minute of the woman's life. Her old father feared for her sanity. Then late one evening she came home, having spent time with a childhood friend. Her father saw that she was radiantly happy. And nine months later...' his voice trailed off.

Jamie had stopped breathing. He sensed that he was teetering on the brink of a yawning black hole. He shook his head to unscramble his thoughts. He focused on the old photograph. He could now see the resemblance between Catriona's son, Joe, and his four year old self. There was a long, long silence between the two men.

Jamie's thoughts were in a whirl. His brain was desperately trying to deny what his eyes could plainly see. He stuttered 'Surely the likeness is just a coincidence... the photographs taken from similar angles, similar poses?'

Dr Fergusson shook his head.

'For a long time I disbelieved what my eyes were plainly telling me because I did not want to suspect my own daughter of infidelity. My suspicions, however, grew and grew. My faith gave me no comfort. I simply had to be sure. So I am ashamed to say that I resorted to unprofessional behaviour for the first and, I hope, last time in my life. I swiped Joe's toothbrush when I was visiting. You dropped in for a whisky. So I kept the glass. I took both to an old friend, a retired analyst. As a favour to me, he used his connections, again totally unprofessionally, to have the glass and toothbrush analysed.'

He delved into the large envelope and fished out a document which he handed to Jamie. With shaking hands Jamie scanned the document which was a DNA report. He could not miss the bold type which pronounced that he, Jamie McHugh, was 98.99% likely to be the biological father of Joe Minton.

Jamie sat there dully, silent. Dr Fergusson continued, a note of bitterness creeping into his voice 'I have known you all your life, Jamie. I loved and respected your grandparents. I still cannot believe that this has happened,' he pointed at the report, 'We will never know how deep was the shadow your careless act cast over an already troubled marriage'.

Jamie eventually found his voice which was thick with emotion, 'I had no idea. Cat never told me. Did she tell Paul, do you think?'

'No, I am certain that she kept it to herself. The question I can't answer is whether he guessed?'

There was another long pause, as Jamie wrestled with the implication of Dr Fergusson's words.

Dr Fergusson broke the silence.

'She never really brought the boy here, save for those few days before the crash. She must have realised that, if Joe was seen on the island, there would be plenty of people who would catch the resemblance and put two and two together.'

He then audibly sighed, as if trying to release the pressure of his distress.

'The few times I visited the family in Glasgow, I found it depressing because the marriage was clearly breaking down. Catriona was wary and on edge. Paul was somehow different...cold and distant. I could see all the happiness that they had shared together slipping away. I thought that it was because Paul was finding it difficult to come to terms with being a father. It didn't occur to me then that he might have found out about your adultery and realised that Cat had been trying to pass off your son as his.'

Jamie started at the ugly word 'adultery', as he had never thought of his brief intimacy with Catriona in those terms before. Yes, he recalled the bitter aftertaste of disquiet at what they had done but, selfishly, he had never given any thought to her husband, Paul. He had been carried away by the moment, believing that he was righting something that had gone wrong between Cat and himself. He now saw himself as crass, irresponsible and utterly selfish.

Jamie groaned as a chill crept over him. The tumble of disorienting flash backs had coalesced into a very dark picture.

'My God, you think Paul did guess and deliberately crashed the car to kill Cat and Joe.'

'And himself'.

'But he must have been insane. You don't kill a beautiful girl or try to kill a child because...'

He could not finish. The logic of what Dr Fergusson was saying was suffocating him.

'You blame me for this tragedy, don't you? This is what this is all about,' he was shouting out in his anguish. He plunged on recklessly, hating the petulance in his voice 'It was something that Cat really wanted. She was the one who wanted to have sex, do you understand me? And now you are telling me that it killed her. What the hell am I supposed to say?'

Dr Fergusson bridled at his words.

Jamie threw the document away from him in his distress, lashing out like a wounded animal.

After another unbearable silence, Dr Fergusson cleared his throat and spoke with difficulty, almost choking on his words 'Whoever was to blame...there are serious consequences...the weight of which must fall on your shoulders. You are Joe's father. He needs to be cared for and...I am too old and ill and, yes, too bitter. He is yours...So take him.' He then added 'If Paul ever recovers...' but did not say any more, merely shook his head. He then called out in a voice hoarse with emotion 'Joe. Come here'.

Jamie started, half stood and was mouthing 'No' as the little boy ran into the room. The boy stopped dead in his tracks as he sensed the charged atmosphere within the room. He looked first at his grandfather for reassurance and then enquiringly at Jamie. 'Who are you?' he said.

***

It was Catriona's brother, Euan, who then stepped into the room to take command of the unravelling situation. He looked like a younger version of his father, the same sweep of hair but, in his case, raven black in colour, so reminiscent of his sister. He had travelled from Ireland for his sister's funeral.

He was brusque and straight to the point. 'My father has told me about you and Cat. It's a mess but I am here to sort out what's best for Joe and for Dad. Both their lives have been turned upside down by all this. Dad can't cope and you can't expect him to at his age. So, I am afraid, it's down to you. No point in prolonging the agony. You have to take on the responsibility now. I have spoken to Finn and Isla, who are expecting Joe tonight.'

He did not look for any response from Jamie who had stiffened at his words.

Jamie was looking towards Dr Fergusson but he had slumped back into his chair and closed his eyes. All his strength was gone. He looked hollow and insubstantial like a bundle of empty clothes discarded on the chair. Jamie wanted to say 'sorry' to him, wanted to say 'goodbye' to him but he could see that it would be unwelcome to a man so utterly lost in the black realms of grief.

Euan had picked up Joe and taken him into the hallway, where he was putting Joe's arms into a navy blue duffle coat before wrapping a large scarf round his neck. All the time he was talking to him in a low reassuring voice. As Jamie walked into the hallway, he heard Euan saying to Joe with a false jollity that he was going on a night time adventure. He would be spending the night at Auntie Isla's house with Esme, Fraser and Lachlan and what fun that would be. He didn't mention Jamie, who was beginning to worry that Joe had no idea who he was. He knew now that he had been judged by the Fergussons. They were leaving it to him to find answers which made sense to a four year old child. They were not going to help him.

Euan stepped outside the cottage and swung Joe onto his shoulders, saying 'Off we go, Tiger' to Joe. He called back over his shoulder to Jamie, 'Joe's bag is underneath the pegs'. Jamie saw a small overnight bag on the floor. Leaning against it was a large teddy bear, dressed in denim shorts with red and blue straps. He picked up both and followed Euan out of the door. He thought he heard someone crying in the kitchen, but he could not be sure.

It was dusk, the light fading into a final hazy greyness before the dark. The temperature had dropped and Jamie found himself shivering. They walked in silence past the last cottage of the row. After a hundred yards the road turned sharply left into a gap in the cliffs and began to climb in long loops towards the top of the cliffs. The road, no more than a faint ribbon in the gathering gloom, skirted the cliff edge for a short distance. It then disappeared inland, towards the wild rugged emptiness of the moors, which haunted the centre of the island. A short distance inland a track branched off the road. It meandered its way up the slope to the Manse, now a black silhouette against a sky rapidly emptying of light. The trees shielding the Manse were dense with crows chattering incessantly about their day's activities. At the last moment before darkness actually fell, they rose with a great clatter into the blackened sky and on mass flew to their roost for the night, roughly two miles away in the woods nestling in Peinchorran hollow. The trio made their silent way up the path.

Finn had been looking out for them and opened the large Manse door as they approached. A warm light spilled out from the door way. Euan took Joe down from his shoulders and handed him to Isla, who had joined Finn at the door. Euan said nothing, just turned on his heels and walked past Jamie without a glance in his direction. Jamie stood awkwardly in the doorway, holding on tightly to the little overnight bag and the large teddy bear. Isla gently placed Joe on the floor and busied herself taking off his coat and scarf, whilst her three children crowded round excitedly jostling one another. Joe was a lonely figure with big solemn eyes, bewildered by the noise and activity around him. Jamie's heart turned over as he watched him. Isla then marshalled the four children towards the staircase, saying it was time for baths and bedtime stories.

She said to Jamie in a matter of fact voice 'I'll shout when it's time for a story for wee Joe and don't forget to bring up teddy'.

Finn put a comforting hand on Jamie's arm and said 'Better get your coat off. I've a big dram waiting for you'.

Finn was as good as his word. When Jamie walked

into the drawing room there was a large tumbler, full to the brim with whisky, ready for him on the coffee table. Since Finn and Isla had moved into the Manse as guardians, they had transformed the austere surroundings into a warm and vibrant home. The wooden settles had been replaced by comfy sofas in bright tartan colours. A large seagrass rug covered most of the stone floor. Colourful seascapes in azure blues, crimson reds and citrus yellows adorned the walls, all of which brought a life and vitality to the room. The paintings had been donated by one of the visiting artists and framed in bleached pine by Finn. James had been pleased to see that Miss May's piano still stood against the far wall. Along the top of the case was a collection of black and white ceramics of differing shapes and sizes, which had turned the piano into a feature of the room rather than an incongruity. He understood that little Esme was learning to play the piano.

Jamie picked up the welcoming tumbler and slumped onto the sofa, which faced towards the piano. He suddenly felt very tired. He took a large sip from the tumbler and breathed in peat and smoke, ancient scents of the land. The heat slid down his throat. Finn sat himself down on the sofa opposite Jamie. He sat distractedly fingering his glass, waiting for Jamie to break the silence but Jamie was too lost in thought. His mind was bubbling over with chaotic images of Catriona, her father, Joe, his grandparents, Arvo and Miss May. They flickered through his mind like an old black and white movie.

Finn was finding the tense silence intolerable. He began to shift uncomfortably as if the sofa was on fire and then, unable to help himself, he blurted out 'I am so sorry, Jamie. I couldn't warn you. Dr Fergusson had asked specifically that I didn't. He was so stricken and has been so ill that I could not refuse him, but it's been sheer torture for Isla and myself. I am truly mortified by what you must view as our disloyalty to you'.

Once he had started to confess, Finn felt impelled to continue, despite the blank response from Jamie, whose thoughts were preoccupied elsewhere.

'We guessed that Joe was your child but did not know whether or how to tell you. Just before the terrible crash, that killed Cat, we paid a surprise visit to her in Glasgow. Isla had been puzzled and upset as to why Cat had become so secretive. Her behaviour had become so strange during the planning application to convert the Boathouse. She was insistent that you were not to be involved. It didn't make any sense because you had found the paintings together. We felt so uncomfortable. It was as if she was trying to drive a wedge between us and to force us into taking her side in some battle of her own making. She was behaving like an adolescent all over again. Remember how she used to be...awkward and belligerent. We felt more and more estranged from her, but did not want to upset her father, so we did nothing.'

Isla appeared and sat herself along side Finn. She took up the story from her husband.

'We were passing through Glasgow on a rare visit to the mainland, and, I will be honest, curiosity got the better of me. I persuaded Finn to drive to Cat's address. We saw Joe playing in the garden and did a double take as Joe is the spitting image of you as a wee boy. We suspected straight away that he was yours and not Paul's. Cat gave us a frosty reception and scarcely concealed her wish to be rid of us. I think she knew we had guessed'.

Finn added 'It was all very sad. This was the last time that we saw Cat alive.'

They fell silent for a moment, clearly distressed that this last occasion had been so cold and unpleasant.

'Seeing Joe made me remember that time in the Boathouse when I found you both together in the chapel with all those flickering candles. Was that when...?' he stopped 'I shouldn't ask, I am sorry'.

Jamie nodded. The image of the two of them together in the chapel was seared into the cortex of his brain. However much he wanted to erase the picture from his memory, he knew he could never forget. Had anything been spontaneous in Catriona's actions that evening? He remembered her urging him up the ladder to the Chapel, the batteries, the matches readily to hand. Had it all been pre-planned? Had he been set up, merely her puppet, her means to the pregnancy she desperately wanted? Had she hated him that much? Then it occurred to him that maybe she had named her son, Joe, after his grandfather, who was also a Joe. Was it a subtle link between her son and his real father, a kind of recognition, an offering of reconciliation?

Isla broke into his muddled thoughts 'Come on, Jamie. It's time for you to read a bedtime story to Joe. You are going to have to start acclimatising Joe to the fact that you are his dad. There isn't a blueprint for any of this, so you will have to play it by ear but, be warned... it is not going to be easy'.

He followed her up the spiral staircase which had been put in to gain access to the attic. The attic had been converted into a spacious bedroom for the children with an indulgently large play area. The play area currently had three small brightly coloured tepees surrounding a round multi-coloured rug in the centre of the room. Bunk beds had been built into the walls and cleverly angled to give each child privacy and their own space. At the far end of the loft a cane chair was hanging from the ceiling, a throw back to the 1960s. The children were in their pyjamas, Isla's children engrossed in fixing a wooden train track. It fitted together like a jigsaw and wound a complicated route all around the loft. Joe sat in front of one of the tepees, quietly watching the others build the track but was too shy to join in.

Isla said very firmly 'No more trains. It's story time now and then bed.' There was mild protest from her children at the mention of bed.

'Come on. No arguments' Isla chivvied, 'It's Joe's turn to pick a book, so Esme would you help him please.'

Esme clearly liked the responsibility she had been given and walked importantly over to Joe and took him by the hand to the bookcase which was stuffed with books of all shapes and sizes. Joe looked uncertainly at the wealth of books facing him but Esme kindly steered him towards a large book with jungle animals on the cover. Meanwhile Isla was orchestrating Jamie and the other children to take up their respective positions, Jamie in the swinging chair and her children on red, yellow and blue bean bags around him. She sat Joe on Jamie's lap causing the chair to swing. Jamie had to keep tight hold of Joe until the rocking steadied. Jamie could feel Joe's fragile frame as he held him and an unexpected tenderness and desire to protect this little child, his child, washed over him. With his arms round Joe for the first time, he held up the book and began to read.

How do you explain to your wife, heavily pregnant with her first child, that you already have a child by another woman; a child who it is now your responsibility and, impliedly, her responsibility to look after; that is, if you remain together. He loved Ellie and he knew that this could blast a seismic hole in their relationship. With a deep sense of foreboding, Jamie had left Joe in the warm care of Finn and Isla, whilst he flew back to Edinburgh to break the news to Ellie and prepare her for the arrival of Joe.

On his way to the airstrip, Jamie stopped off at the small craft hut, painted bright blue, which was nestled in the hillside on the far side of bay. He bought Ellie a hand knitted sweater in grey and cream, which he knew she would love, and a large box of heart shaped, home baked shortbread. Peace offerings, foolish really, but he just could not turn up empty handed and deliver bad news cold. On the flight he rehearsed in his mind what he was going to say to Ellie in ten, twenty different ways, all of which ended up sounding like the lamest of excuses. He was so distracted that, when he arrived at his own doorstep, he rang the bell rather than using his door key. He felt disorientated as he heard Ellie approaching the door. After a momentary surprise, she threw her arms round him in the warmest of welcomes, which made him feel even more miserable and ashamed.

In the living room he immediately handed her the sweater and shortbread, which, as he had anticipated, delighted her. She was trying on the sweater, as he busied himself in the kitchen making a pot of tea. He lingered over the ritual of making the tea, carefully spooning fresh Earl Grey leaves into the strainer inside the teapot. He poured the hot water until it covered the leaves in the strainer. He then swirled it around in the pot before pouring the tea into the small, earthenware cups, which they had bought from a specialist tea shop on the Lothian Road. As he came down the steps into the living room, balancing a bamboo tray, Ellie was happily showing off her new sweater, asking him what he thought. He said 'It looks great' but distractedly and without his usual warm appreciation. He then solemnly asked her to sit down. She did as he asked and sank back onto the sofa, hushed by his sudden sombre tone. She watched him attentively with a quizzical look as he placed the tea cups from the tray onto the coffee table and slowly unwrapped the box of shortbread, which he left open on the table.

He stood there for a time, hesitating but, when he finally found the words, his confession tumbled from him like water gushing from a breaking dam...how he had betrayed their relationship, how he had had carelessly fathered a child. He did not put any blame on Catriona, although he was now certain that she had manipulated him. That felt like a poor excuse and anyway he would not sully her memory. So he ended portraying himself in the worst possible light. Ellie did not interrupt his abject confession. At one point he wanted to get the DNA report to show her, but she merely shook her head. She did, however, look long and hard at a photograph of Joe. He ended pathetically with 'I have only ever loved you'. Although he wanted to invest this declaration with all the profound sincerity he could muster, it sounded hollow, even to his ears.

Ellie did not respond but mechanically reached for a biscuit, which she dipped into the mug of tea. After a while, she said in a monotone 'I have news too. I have had the second scan and we are having a little girl'. He automatically went to hug her but she pushed him away, saying 'I need time, Jamie, to think through all of this...'

For a day or two there was silence between them. Slowly Ellie processed what Jamie had said and its consequences for herself and her unborn baby. Instinctively Ellie had always disliked the thought of Catriona, even though she had never met her. She had been jealous of her for years, having convinced herself that Catriona had been Jamie's first love. Jamie had never said as much but he always talked so warmly of her and of their shared childhood. He would, however, have been surprised, if she had suggested to him that he had more than friendly feelings towards Catriona.

On the third day of purgatory, it was her turn to tell Jamie to sit on the sofa, which he did with trepidation. He was frightened that she was going to announce the end of their relationship. Very quietly she told him that she had been working through her feelings, trying to give herself space and perspective. She could not forgive his disloyalty, although she recognised that his intimate relationship with Catriona pre-dated their marriage. She knew that she had a Gallic tendency towards jealousy but then had she not been right to be jealous of his friendship with Catriona? She could perhaps sense things that he could not see for himself. His intimacy with Catriona had been a bitter body blow to her feelings, but she did accept that it was only on one occasion. She could see that his relationship with herself was fundamentally different...much stronger, more enduring, more committed, truly loving. The hard question she had to ask herself was 'Could she trust him again?' and, after deep soul searching, her answer was 'Yes.' Ultimately their marriage was worth saving for the sake of their unborn child, who had been conceived with their deepest love and longing for a family together.

She then looked at him fully in the eyes and said 'I love you, I love our baby and I will do my best to love and protect your son, Joe, as part of you, and embrace him as part of our family'.

Jamie broke down in tears when she gave her verdict on their future together. He was an extraordinarily lucky man and he knew it. He had been given a magnanimous reprieve by a woman, who was bigger and better than he was. He also knew that he was on probation as a husband and a father.

They flew out to the island together and spent a couple of days with Finn and Isla so as to get to know Joe better before embarking upon a new life as a family in Edinburgh. They found to their dismay that Joe had become a frozen child. He was badly traumatised and had closed in on himself, as a way of dealing with all the sudden changes and losses in his life. Had it not been for the calming experience of Isla and Finn and the lively presence of their three children, it would have been difficult, if not impossible, for Jamie and Ellie to know how to break down his sullen wall of indifference. It brought home to them the enormity of the task ahead of them. It was going to take a great deal of work on their part before he could trust them.

What in fact broke the ice was the birth of his half sister, Georgette. There was an instant rapport between the two siblings. She was a beautiful baby with dark curly hair, hazel brown eyes and the deepest of contralto gurgles. For Joe it was love at first sight. He marvelled at her little hands and little feet and immediately was proprietorial and protective towards her. He would talk to her happily for hours, telling her adventure stories about a spaceship which he had called JG 77 after their initials. Georgie loved all the attention and would vigorously kick her arms and legs and squeal with delight. It became part of their family history that she smiled at Joe first, of which he was inordinately proud. Gradually as he played a part in her care, he opened up to Jamie and Ellie. It was like a slow unfurling of an angry, tightly closed fist into an open hand. When he finally called Jamie 'Daddy', Jamie could not help himself. He spontaneously hugged him and, in his joy and relief, raised him high in his arms, spinning him round and round in a wild dance.

***

It was several weeks later that Jamie found himself in Glasgow. His practice was handling its first prestigious project for a new computing centre within the University Campus. The Centre was being built on the site of a demolished 1960s building behind the Informatics Centre. The brief was to accommodate over a hundred computer terminals, top lit to avoid light falling onto computer screens. Longitudinally, within a simple barn like space, he had designed four of his signature tiers bisected by a central staircase. He had modelled the overhead lighting on that used in the Vanhoven Computer Building in San Francisco. Over the last few years he had tendered for several important public schemes and, though his designs had been short listed each time, this was the first project which had matured into a contract for the actual build. Jamie was excited but under considerable pressure to succeed, if the practice was to have any chance of developing into a major architectural player in Scotland.

He had been on site all week. The build was progressing well and his university client was pleased but pushing for completion. Jamie had been very focused, eating and sleeping the project, and had expended a lot of nervous energy. It had left him feeling drained at the end of the week. He was looking forward to his weekend break at home with Ellie and the children in Edinburgh.

It was late afternoon as he started to drive out of Glasgow and cursed to himself as he immediately hit the long tail back of Friday night rush hour traffic. He was crawling like a tortoise past the Kelvin Infirmary Hospital in a slow moving queue. On the spur of the moment he decided to drive into the large Hospital car park. He needed to get out of the monotonous line of cars for a few minutes and try to recover his sorely tried patience. Miraculously there was a parking space not far from the main entrance. He decided to take ten minutes out. Then suddenly, on a whim, which he later could not understand, he decided that he would go and see for himself Catriona's husband, Paul. He had been a long term patient in the Kelvin Infirmary for the many months since the crash. Notwithstanding his comatose state, Paul had caused much anguish in Jamie's life, swelling into monstrous proportions in Jamie's imagination as the killer of Catriona. He dominated his dreams and turned them into nightmares, which left Jamie soaking and drained on waking. Maybe, if he saw Paul as a person rather than a monster, things would come back into proportion.

The Kelvin Infirmary is one of those huge, sprawling modern hospitals with endless corridors throbbing to the insistent march of bustling nurses, busy doctors, scuttling porters, hobbling patients and bewildered, lost visitors. Jamie joined the wandering throng of visitors and after a number of enquires and misdirections found his way to Ward 623 on the fourth floor. There the coma victims were laid out like corpses in a succession of curtained bays, each patient wired up to a battery of bleeping, winking instruments. A nurse was sitting at a central station, staring at a computer. She eventually took notice of Jamie and directed him to the penultimate bay on the left.

As he peered into the bay, he saw a figure lying inert on the bed with a spider's web of lines hooking him up to bags suspended from metal poles on either side of the bed. Wires trailed over the bed to a large oblong instrument box with a blinking screen. The screen cast a ghostly green light over the cubicle and gave a spectral hue to the immobile face just visible above the taut line of the bedclothes. He looked like a recumbent statue in the crypt of a church, immovable for centuries, with deep shadows accentuating the carved features of his face. As Jamie stood by the curtain, mesmerised by the sepulchral scene, someone stirred on the opposite side of the bed to the instrument box. Jamie peered into the gloom and saw a woman sitting on a chair beside the bed.

'I am so sorry to disturb you' he stuttered. 'I came to see Paul' was his embarrassed explanation. The woman rose and walked towards him. She took him by the arm and led him out of the cubicle. She was a small, thick set woman in her late thirties with savagely cropped blond hair. Her unremarkable features were dominated by a pair of over sized spectacles. What startled the eye was the exotic garment she was wearing. Jamie was not entirely sure whether she was wearing a coat or a cloak or some sort of poncho. It was made from from a tapestry like material in a swirl of blue and orange colours with a large red and green fringe. It gave her otherwise owlish presence a sense of quixotic drama.

'I'm Janie, Paul's elder sister. Forgive me taking you away but I don't like talking in front of Paul as if he's not there. He can hear everything, you know. Are you a friend of Paul?'

'I'm Jamie McHugh. I was a friend of Catriona and...'

She interrupted 'Oh, you are the one looking after Joe.'

He nodded.

'How is Joe? I'm sorry I've not been in touch but I live and work abroad, you see. This is the first time I have been able to get some time off work to come to the UK to see Paul since the funeral.'

Her voice trailed off with a heavy sigh 'I guess you can say I have been in denial, as well as a long way from Scotland. It's a poor explanation, I know.'

She shrugged, 'I look at Paul and just feel guilty'.

'Joe is fine. It took him a while to settle but he is OK now...' Jamie said but she interrupted him again, as if her mind was elsewhere and she was not really taking in what he was saying.

'You know, I've been looking at my brother just now, wishing him to die. That is such a bad thing to say, I know, but it's true. There is nothing for him, absolutely nothing except just lying there like a corpse. Why don't they switch the damn machine off'?' she implored Jamie with surprising vehemence. Clutching at Jamie's arm she pulled him away from the cubicle, saying 'Let's go for a coffee and talk' in a tone that was an order rather than a request.

Jamie juggled two piping hot coffees to the table, where Paul's sister and her flamboyant coat had stationed themselves with a view of the cafeteria. Jamie noticed with a sigh that the décor was intended to be minimalist but merely looked cold and unwelcoming with its fake marble tables and uncomfortable skeletal chairs. On one wall there was an abstract mural made up of light blue, shiny tiles across which red paint had been randomly splattered. As he was sitting down, Janie leaned over the table towards him and whispered that she had deliberately chosen this table, 'so they could talk'.

He sat down opposite her and for a difficult moment or two they stared down at the steaming coffee and the fake marble table. Janie suddenly started to talk in her tense, distracted manner as if in a rush to unburden herself.

'Do you know anything about my family? No, of course you don't'.

She paused for a moment and began tracing the pattern of the marble veining with her finger like a young child learning to read the words in a book.

Sighing deeply, she said 'We are a cursed family or to be more exact the male members of my family are cursed. They carry from father to son a genetic condition, Jagerdorff Syndrome, which slowly destroys their bodies and their minds. There is no cure. I cannot begin to describe to you the horror of watching someone you love disintegrate until they cease to be a person; first, it was my father and then it was my youngest brother, Billy. What upset me the most was how the disease radically changed their personalities. The medics were at a loss, wrongly diagnosing this and that. It was not until the post mortem of Billy that this rare disease was identified as the cause of death. As a doctor, Paul understood immediately the consequences for himself but, like most mortals facing a dreadful death, he continued to hope he would be spared from the disease. But in the end the 'not knowing' became unbearable and he had himself tested. I begged him not to do it but he was determined to do it. And inevitably he was given his death sentence but with no means of knowing how long it would be before the disease would eat him up.'

She paused for a moment before continuing.

'He never told Catriona because he did not know how to and was anxious that it would crush her mentally. I was forbidden from telling anyone. So we continued to keep it a terrible family secret and, silently from the sidelines, I watched it destroy his marriage and then destroy his wife. He couldn't have children, you see, and pass on the curse and he couldn't tell her why'.

She looked up at him and searched his eyes for understanding.

'You do see, don't you? How could he take the risk of passing onto a son a fate worse than death and perpetuating the curse into the future? So when Catriona unexpectedly became pregnant with Joe, his obsession with the curse got out of control and turned him...' she hesitated, '...Quite, quite insane. Although he presented a calm, controlled appearance to the world, I could see that the illness and the madness were worming their venom into his very soul and yet I still said nothing. I just couldn't bear to see another brother destroyed and so I turned my back and left for a new life as far away as possible.'

She gave him a piercing look directly into his eyes. 'So I am as guilty as you are for what happened to Catriona.'

Jamie started at this last comment but she carried on before he could get out a word.

'I came back for Catriona's funeral. I believed that Joe was Paul's son and I wanted to make amends by offering to help care for him. I was staying at Dr Fergusson's cottage and was in the kitchen with Joe, when you came to the cottage. I heard every word that Catriona's father said to you.'

A note of bitterness crept into her voice.

'How ironic it all is! Joe is your son, not Paul's. Joe doesn't carry my family's curse after all. Paul still doesn't know. He never imagined that Catriona could have been unfaithful to him and believed one hundred per cent that Joe was his son. He became frantic that he had prolonged the curse by fathering a son and was absolutely terrified for his son's future. He blamed Catriona for having the child. It drove him mad and ultimately dangerous. I should have said something but I couldn't break the family code. So I let it happen. I ought to have told Dr Fergusson the truth too. But, do you see? I couldn't'.

She appeared to finish and pushed her untouched coffee away from her as if to signal she had come to the end of what she wanted to say.

Jamie did not react but sat as if turned into stone. For the second time in his life he had sat through a harrowing monologue, which had ripped him apart and left him numb, empty and lost.

She plainly had a need to fill the silence, as she carried on heedless of the impact she was having with her words.

'Maybe you can understand now why I wish him dead. The disease hasn't stopped just because he is lying there in a coma. It goes on and on and on, eating his humanity away. All I could see today as I looked at him were agony and hopelessness. Do you understand...I do not want him to wake up and face such an unimaginably cruel death. But I haven't the courage to turn off the switch, you see. That's why I have broken my promise and told you the truth. I know I shouldn't ask but could... would you do it and stop this nightmare for my family?'

She asked this, a little too eagerly.

It took him a moment to understand that she was actually asking him to end her brother's life, to turn off the life support machine. At the same time, he realised that this was a serious and desperate request and, in his shock, his first thought was 'Why me?' An instinctive horror kicked in and he shook his head vigorously as if he was warding off a stinging wasp.

'No, no. I can't, I absolutely can't take a life. I am very very sorry for you both but I can't.'

She visibly deflated but only for a fraction of a second before she stood up abruptly and began to walk away briskly from the table. There was a brief backward glance as she tossed an after thought to him 'I am glad Joe is fine. You need to keep him tight.' She shrugged and then her colourful coat disappeared through the swinging doors and the cafeteria returned to its soulless uniformity.

Jamie did not move. He was asking himself 'Did that really just happen? Was I hallucinating?' As a tidal wave of anguish washed over him, he knew he had to see Paul again, though he had no idea as to why this felt so imperative. He retraced his steps to Paul's bay and sat down gingerly on the chair by the side of the bed, where Paul lay as still as a corpse. As he looked at Paul's waxen, parchment face, deeply etched with lines of grief and pain, he no longer saw the inhuman ogre, who had waylaid his dreams night after night. He now understood that the picture was far more complex and multi-layered than he had ever imagined. Yes, Paul had killed Cat in a moment of insanity, for which Jamie could never forgive him, but this insanity was the cruel and agonising consequence of a terrible disease. Paul was not a monster but a desperately lonely human being in the grip of a cruel and remorseless fate. No imagination could plumb the depths of the horror churning on an endless loop through his damaged mind. Jamie found himself saying again and again 'I am so sorry. I am so sorry,' however brittle and inadequate he knew these words were.

He was brought back to reality by the vibrations of his mobile phone. He mechanically took it out of his pocket and saw that there was a message from Ellie, asking where he was and when was he likely to get home. He inwardly groaned. What was he going to say to her? He had no credible explanation as to why he had gone to the hospital in the first place. He had felt for a long time that he was merely a puppet being dangled over one precipice after another by a sadistically amused manipulator. But he could hardly tell her that. Without clearly thinking things through, he rashly decided that he was not going to tell her anything about his bizarre encounter with Paul's sister. He was not going to run the risk of reopening old wounds. 'Better to lick the new wounds and just go home and forget it', he thought as he got into his car.

On a Thursday several months later he stepped out into an early December morning clothed in a watery blue sky and pale lemon sunlight. The glimpses of the sun gave an energising illusion of warmth, even though the pavement was lightly frosted. Old Hailes Row was a quiet backwater thanks to no-through traffic but, being in the centre of the city, it did not escape from the lines of tightly parked cars on either side of the road. Parking his own car often required considerable ingenuity.

He noticed a large black car, which was badly parked opposite his house, its wheels more on the pavement than on the street. As he looked at the car, an involuntary shudder, out of nowhere, ran through his body. As if someone had turned on a harsh spotlight, the familiar street scene turned into a surreal, topsy turvy world where the colours were so pin sharp that he had to shut his eyes to avoid the pain to his retina. His legs felt unpleasantly heavy and numb. He stamped one foot after the other to feel some connection to the ground. This sense of other worldliness lasted only for a second or two before everything righted itself again. He shook his head to clear the fog in his mind.

With an irritated shrug of his shoulders, he carried on with his usual routine of fetching the daily newspapers and a bag of croissant to kick start another busy day. He walked very briskly to and from the newspaper shop, his token exercise. He had a daily exercise regime worked out in his head, which involved cycling and running, and rowing, but, in reality, he had no time to put any of it into practice.

He was quite warm from the brisk walk as he turned back into Old Hailes Row but, as he approached his front door, he began to shiver again. He tried to shrug it off, got the key out of his pocket and was putting it in the lock, when he sensed something hostile lurking immediately behind him. He whipped round in fright. There was nothing there. The street was empty save for the lines of parked cars.

Once inside his house he felt immediate relief but found that he could not shake this strange feeling loose. As a result, the next few mornings he was very wary as he left the house. It is funny how once you notice something, you keep noticing it. Whenever he looked at the parked cars, there standing out from the crowd was the black car, more often than not parked directly opposite his house. He was becoming increasingly curious about the black car. He knew most of the makes of his neighbours' cars and he did not recognise this black car as belonging to anyone he knew. Nor was he was aware of any newcomer to the street, which could, maybe, account for a new vehicle. As space was at such a premium, he began to resent this big beast of a car as an unwelcome intruder selfishly taking up too much space on their narrow, little street. Even when he was in the house, he found himself staring up and down the street from the window, checking where the black car was.

***

About a week later he was taking Joe ice skating for a pre Christmas treat. That Christmas an ice rink had been erected to encircle Melville's Column in St Andrew Square. For several years, the rink had become a traditional part of the Christmas scene in the centre of Edinburgh with its skaters, of all shapes, sizes and skill, whirling round the column, whilst Henry Dundas, 1st Viscount Melville, looked down from his towering height of 45 metres. Joe was feverishly excited, as it was his first time. In his eagerness he was tugging at his father, who was struggling with the zip of his wax jacket by the front door. They almost fell out of the door into the street. Laughing they set off together with Joe dancing up and down by his father's side. As they were crossing the street, Jamie saw the black car. Joe suddenly stopped in the middle of the street and hung back. Clutching onto his father's leg, he let out a shrill cry 'I don't like that car. I don't like it.'Jamie took a good, hard look through the passenger windows of the car but the windows were so darkly tinted that he could not see anyone inside. It could have been empty.

'Come on. It's OK' he said to Joe in a gentle but firm voice so as to encourage him to walk on but Joe still resisted. He went limp as young children sometimes do when reluctant to do something. Jamie had to lift him to his feet and half pulled, half carried him past the car until they were round the corner.

Once the car was out of sight, Joe's spirits revived almost instantaneously and he began to fizz with excitement again. This increased exponentially when they reached the Square and he saw the throng of skaters. The experienced skaters were spinning and twirling in the razzle, dazzle lights in tune to the blearing beat of the music. The inexperienced clung onto the railing as they slithered treacherously on their unaccustomed blades. Jamie hired one of the waist high plastic penguins designed for the younger children. He settled Joe at the front of the penguin on its large feet and told Joe to hang onto its outstretched wings. Pushing the penguin from behind, he then skated quite fast into the flow of skaters, skilfully swerving between the hesitant and the unsteady. Joe, standing at the front of the penguin, shouted out in elation as they whizzed round and round the rink. A bridge, at one point, spanned the rink, as a viewing point for those just wanting to watch the skaters. As Joe looked up, he saw the spectators on the bridge. He waved enthusiastically at them and smiled broadly when the waves were returned. Jamie did not notice this exchange because he was too busy concentrating on keeping his footing. Neither of them noticed the figure on the bridge who had been watching Joe intently and had not raised his hand to wave.

When they got back home, the black car was no longer there.

***

The next day the black car was back. Jamie saw it from the window; big and menacing like a fat spider waiting for the touch of juicy prey in its web. He stormed out of the house and ran over to the car. He knocked impatiently on the passenger window and then tried to peer through the tinted window. There was someone sitting there, completely still. Jamie sensed a malevolent presence which had not only frightened his son but was now doing a good job of frightening him too. There was no response from inside the car. This further infuriated Jamie who began tugging roughly at the door handle. It did not budge. It was locked. It took all Jamie's self control not to kick at the door in his frustration. He hammered repeatedly on the passenger window with both hands, shouting 'Go away' to whoever was immobile and silent inside.

Ellie came running out of the house. 'Jamie, what on earth are you doing?' She pulled him away from the car. 'Stop it, just stop it' she said, both alarmed and horrified by the public spectacle Jamie was making of himself on their street. Jamie's burst of nervous energy was spent. Still shaking, he allowed Ellie to lead him back into their house.

In the sitting room he saw Joe kneeling on the floor beside the coffee table, wholly absorbed in colouring a picture in a large book with red and yellow crayons. Jamie bent down and kissed him on top of his head. Ellie said 'What on earth was that about?'

He sat down heavily on the sofa.'I think we are being stalked' he said.

'Stalked!' Ellie cried out in disbelief.

'The black car. It's been there for days lurking like a black slug'.

'Jamie, you are not making any sense. It's a car, just a car.'Ellie shook her head, 'I don't believe this'.

'Joe sensed it too' Jamie said, as if trying to add weight to his argument.

'He's five years old. You are thirty five. You have just made an utter spectacle of yourself. Thank God no one got out of the car. I honestly believe you would have hit them and we would have the police at our door by now.'

'Police, of course. I should report this to the Police' Jamie said distractedly.

'Report what? A car parked on a street! You don't even know the registration number.' Jamie started at this and, seeing his reaction, Ellie threw her arms in the air in frustration 'Don't even think of going outside again to get the number. The Police would think you were mad. Come on now, you have work to do or have you forgotten?'

Ellie could be forceful and quietly effective when roused and she deployed all of her skills in calming

Jamie down and successfully bringing him back to earth. Privately, however, she was unnerved by Jamie's uncharacteristic irrationality. She was puzzled and uneasy as to what it was that had so spooked him. It was so contrary to his usual demeanour of gentle dreaminess, which was what she loved most about him. She knew that he had an uncanny way of sensing things which others could not. She respected that but she was beginning to worry that this second sight was slipping out of control into paranoia.

The next day the black car was parked at the end of Old Hailes Row on the opposite side of the street.

'It's him. He's come back', Jamie whispered to himself in. He pushed a notebook in his coat pocket as he left the house. He crossed the street and stood in front of the car, ostentatiously writing down the registration number, QY 65 PBM, in the notebook. He was pretty sure that there was someone sitting in there, watching him. He hoped whoever it was would now back off, knowing that he had taken down the registration number.

This tactic seemed to work for a day or two but then, like a recurring nightmare, the black car was again parked directly opposite his house. Something inside Jamie snapped again, when he saw it. He grabbed his coat and marched in anger to the nearest police station, which was in a red stone Victorian building, three streets away, on Geachan Street.

As he walked into the poorly lit lobby, he saw a uniformed officer sitting behind a counter which was protected by a large sheet of reinforced glass. A woman with badly dyed black hair, tatty plastic bags at her feet, was monopolising the counter. She was bending down with difficulty to shout through the semi circle of holes which pierced the lower edge of the glass partition so as to allow communication.

On the left hand side of the lobby there was a bench, where an old man dressed in a greasy coat was sitting, his head lolling backwards against the dirty cream wall. His mouth was wide open and was displaying a row of cracked greenish teeth. His chest was wheezing like a steam train and he was giving off such a pungent stench that Jamie sat himself gingerly on the very edge of the bench as far away as he could from the ravaged old man.

The woman was gabbling in an agitated rush of words at the officer, who was nodding periodically but had plainly stopped listening to her tirade some time before. The Officer's red hair had receded well beyond the crown of his head, leaving him with a prominent, bulging forehead, which shone like polished stone under the strip lighting. A pair of reading glasses were perched precariously at the end of his long nose, over which he gazed at the woman with bored eyes. Eventually she ran out of steam and the officer mumbled something to her, which caused her to turn away sharply from the counter. She picked up her multiple plastic bags and struggled towards the door. Jamie opened the door for her and watched her briefly as she hobbled down the street, still shaking her head and muttering.

As the old man was out for the count, Jamie took his place at the counter. There was a piece of white cardboard stuck on the inside of the glass with the words 'PS Jack Dunnimore' in black biro. Sergeant Dunnimore was sipping coffee from a styrene cup. A half eaten doughnut lay on a paper bag to his right. He sighed heavily and then gave Jamie a quizzical gaze over the top of his glasses. Jamie's anger had largely dissipated by the time he had sat down in the dismal lobby and he was beginning to regret his decision. He swallowed hard and said 'My family is being stalked'.

Sergeant Dunnimore said wearily 'Right, you had better give me your details. Name. Address.' He brushed doughnut sugar from the topmost sheet of paper. After laboriously writing down Jamie's details, he looked up and said 'So who is stalking you?'

'I don't know who he is,' Jamie said, realising how lame he sounded, 'I can see this figure sitting in a black car outside my house, watching me and my family. He's there day after day. It's intimidating. You can't see who it is because the windows are heavily tinted but there is someone there, watching. It frightens my little boy who is only five years old'.

'Is the car parked there 24/7?'

'No, it comes and goes'.

'Is there restricted parking on your street?'

'No'

'Is he obstructing your house in any way?'

'No, it's hard to explain. He just sits there watching. It's very unsettling.' Jamie was floundering, as he saw how bizarre his fears must sound to this hard bitten desk sergeant. How could he explain the overpowering sense of menace emanating from a stationary car.

He tried one last tack, 'I have the registration number, so you can trace whoever it is'.

Sergeant Dunnimore shook his head, 'No, no. We can't start tracing car owners for no reason. Last time I looked, it wasn't a crime to park a car where there is unrestricted parking and no obstruction. It's probably someone who parks there for a quiet kip away from the wife. I wouldn't worry about it.'

When Jamie began to remonstrate, the Officer, with an even heavier sigh, said 'Look, I can't give you a crime number, as there hasn't been a crime, but I will make a note of your complaint in the daily computer log. I can't do any more'.

Jamie took those words as a dismissal and apologised for wasting the Officer's time. The irony was lost on PS Dunnimore. He had already turned his attention back to the doughnut, from which he now took a large bite with a look of satisfaction.

Jamie recounted to Ellie what had happened, when he got back home. She shrugged unsympathetically, saying 'What did you expect? I told you it would be a stupid thing to do'.

***

The following day Ellie was distressed when she overheard Jamie telephoning the school and lying that Joe was too unwell to attend. Ellie told him that it was wrong to keep Joe away from school when he was perfectly well, but then added in a bitter tone, 'Of course, it is your business. He is your child, not mine'. This last comment upset Jamie because this was the first time that Ellie had ever referred to Joe in this way. This spat, however, did not prevent Jamie putting off a visit by his parents, which was scheduled for the Saturday. They were going to take their grandchildren to the Zoo and had been planning it for weeks. Ellie knew how disappointed they would be and berated him for his selfishness, saying that she was shocked that he could be so cruel to them. She angrily told him that she could not understand him any more. She was at a loss. His normally sunny disposition had turned dark and suspicious and she was finding it difficult to cope with his restless moods. He had always been the steady, strong partner who gave her stability and confidence. She now feared that she was losing him to something indefinable and infinitely slippery. Every five minutes he was staring out of the window with a haggard look on his face.

As Jamie checked the street for the umpteenth time, Ellie suggested in desperation that maybe it was time to get away for a few days as a family. Her private reasoning was that, if they could at least put some distance between Jamie and his irrational fear, he may be able to relax and recover his equilibrium. So she was pleased when Jamie immediately rang Finn to see if Lur Beag was free, which fortunately it was. Ellie and the children had never been to the cottage. The last time Jamie and Ellie had been on the island was their traumatic stay with Finn and Isla at Tarkavay House, when Ellie was introduced to Joe for the first time. It had not been a happy time but Ellie still had a hankering for a visit to the cottage, which she knew was such a special place for Jamie and one that she wanted to experience for herself.

Finn promised to get the cottage warm and stocked with food, ready for their visit. On hearing the delight in Finn's voice Jamie felt a flood of relief wash over him at the prospect of returning to Lur Beag, which had always been his refuge as a child.

They quickly packed the car and drove out of Edinburgh with Jamie looking constantly in the rear view mirror. Even though they had set off before the morning rush hour, he was forced to drive at a snail's pace through the West End and past Corstorphine due to the endless roadworks clogging up the streets. He got on to the airport road, where things cleared a little and he was able to pick up a bit of speed. As he was approaching the RBS metal bridge, he checked his rear mirror. The vehicle behind him was black.

'Surely, it can't be the black car', he said to himself and his mouth felt very dry. Instinctively he began pressing down hard on the accelerator.

'You're speeding,' Ellie said sharply, mindful of the two children strapped into car seats in the rear.

'There's a black car behind us' said Jamie, nodding backwards with his head.

Ellie looked round, peering out of the rear window.

'What? Jamie, it's just an ordinary car,' she said decisively.

Jamie clenched his jaw and looked fixedly ahead. The next time he steeled himself to look in the rear view mirror, there was no black vehicle. With an inward sigh of relief, he assumed that it must have turned off at the airport.

***

Once on the M9 Jamie was making good speed. However, near Falkirk, they could see in the distance the Kelpies, distinctive horse head sculptures, 30 metres high, dominating the horizon. Joe became so excited that Ellie suggested that they make a short detour. Whilst Ellie stayed behind with Georgie in the car, Jamie and Joe joined the straggle of families making their way along a sandy track across the The Helix parkland, which lay beside the extension of the Forth and Clyde Canal. Suddenly ahead of them the heads of the two gigantic steel horses reared up against the grey clouds; one looking pensively downwards and the other tossing his head skywards with wild eyes and flaring nostrils. Joe was stunned and momentarily frightened by their sheer scale. Jamie picked him up and swept him up onto his shoulders. They proceeded at a stately march towards the specially constructed lock and basin, where the sculptures had been built of structural steel with hollow stainless steel cladding.

Joe could only gasp in awe as they drew closer. The Kelpies were so enormous that he had to throw his head right back, squinting against the light, to see the topmost part of their heads disappearing into the sky. He clamoured to be put down and then wanted to walk round the huge circular bases of the horses. His father told him about the sculptor, Andy Scott, and explained that The Kelpies were mythical water horses. Joe went up to the neck of the pensive horse and stroked it tenderly.

Up close he was delighted to see that the steel was perforated with multiple slits, through which he could peek inside the vast hollow neck of the horse. He beckoned to his father and they both peered through the holes into the cavernous interior, their hands braced against the steel frame. Jamie smiled to see the visitors on the opposite side likewise peering into the shadowy cathedral like space in wonder. For a second a pair of opposing eyes stared straight at him through the mesh of steel. It gave him a jolt. An illustration from his father's copy of Dumas' 'The Man in the Iron Mask' flashed into his mind, a pair of desperate eyes staring out of a hideous iron mask. The thought of a suffocating iron mask encasing his head, trapping and choking him, had haunted him as a child and led to many a nightmare. He had always hated the idea of his hands touching the cold iron of the mask, unable to feel the warm flesh of his face. These childhood fears were rudely brought into the present, as he again relived that terrifying feeling of claustrophobia. The steel beneath his hands seemed to break free from the horse's skeleton and slowly form round his head in a tight fitting mask, forcing his eyes to stare out through the narrowest of slits. He shivered involuntarily and sprang back from the horse's neck as if he had been electrocuted. Joe looked round at him and gave him a puzzled look. Jamie jerked his head and said abruptly 'Come on. We have to get back to the car'. He lifted Joe on to his shoulders and hurried back to the car park He was discomforted that he had let Joe witness his reaction to an old fear.

Jamie was briefly hindered from exiting the car park by pedestrians meandering in the car lane. It allowed him a moment to scan the lines of parked cars. Was that a black car over on the left or was he imagining things? He did not dare ask Ellie to look and he had no further time to check himself, as the exit cleared and he was finally able to drive out of the park. When he checked in the rear view mirror, he was greatly relieved to see that he had not been followed by any vehicle out of the car park.

***

In the early afternoon, as they approached the Pass of Glencoe, the sky began to close in and take on a sulphurous sheen. Heavy storm clouds were massing, turning the sky into patches of black, purple and dark blue like multiple bruises. The road twisted through the bleak landscape of Rannoch Moor, carpeted in brackish heather and pockmarked with black lochans and a scatter of tiny islands, on which solitary trees lodged precariously. The gathering storm appeared to have deterred local traffic and for mile after mile Jamie had the road to himself. He was half listening to the car radio. Ellie and the children were fast asleep.

The rain began to pour and needles of water hammered against the windscreen, sending the wipers into a frenzy of activity. Vicious winds thundering across the moor rocked the car, which suddenly felt very fragile. Jamie slowed to a crawl and put on his headlights on full beam, trying to penetrate the murky gloom. He was entering the narrow defile of Glencoe with its grim grandeur and wild and precipitous mountains. His hands gripped the steering wheel, his head strained forward as he struggled to see the bends in the road ahead. The rear wipers momentarily cleared the rear windscreen and he became aware of headlights flickering in the far distance behind him. He saw a lay-by and decided to hunker down there until the worst of the storm passed by.

The steep walls of the mountains loomed around him, dramatic, sheer and ominous in the unnatural darkness of the storm. The mountains had witnessed the grisly massacre of the MacDonalds during the Jacobite Rebellion, the stories of which had filled his imagination as a child, sharing, as he did, a distant kinship with the clan. The sense of desolation was overwhelming. He felt that the rocks themselves were impregnated with sorrow. He imagined, for a moment, that he could hear in the keening wind the plaintive echo of ghostly bagpipes playing a lament for his murdered kin. He shuddered. This was not the happiest place for someone with a vivid imagination to wait out a storm.

Before he had turned off the engine, the car was suddenly illuminated by the full headlights of a vehicle which had driven into the lay-by immediately behind him. The flood of light was dazzling and so intrusive that it momentarily blinded him. Cursing, he shielded his eyes with his hands. In the harsh glare Ellie and the children began to stir in their sleep. The driver was showing no signs of turning off the beam, notwithstanding that it must have been obvious that the light was blinding everyone in Jamie's car. Jamie was puzzled and then angry. Was the light being deliberately used to intimidate them? The thought had no sooner crossed his mind than panic kicked in. He slammed on the door safety locks, revved the engine, which had been idling, and, without daring a backward glance, accelerated out of the lay-by. Adrenaline was pumping through his body. He knew that he was driving too fast for the road conditions but fear of pursuit had given him a grim, gimlet like focus. Fortunately there was no oncoming traffic and he managed to keep a tight control of the car, as it skidded round the sharper bends. The jolting of the car and the squealing of the tyres had woken Ellie from her sleep and, as she realised what was happening, she cried out in horror. At her cry an image of Catriona, her lips drawn back screaming, scorched his mind like a lightening bolt. He instantly slowed down but could not resist a backward glance in the rear view mirror. There were no following headlights. His thundering heart beat began to calm down. He stole a look at Ellie who was ashen and shaking, her face turned to stone. He murmured 'Sorry' but knew that he could not begin to explain. They drove on in silence, Ellie angry and tense at his side.

It was only in the early evening when they were in the queue for the ferry that he finally began to relax. Ellie broke her silence, but only to give full vent to her pent up anger at his insanity and irresponsibility towards her and the children. 'Did he really want Joe to survive a car crash only to be killed in a crazy crash of his making' she said sharply, her barb striking home with devastating force.

He did not try to defend himself or his actions. Ellie was justifiably annoyed. He had panicked and endangered his family because of an uncontrollable feeling that they were being threatened. At the time the sense of menace had been so overmastering and real that he felt he had no other course than to act immediately to escape from the danger. With hindsight, he realised, only too starkly, that, instead of protecting his family, he had nearly killed them by driving like a maniac.

***

The large, ungainly hulk of the ferry docked with practised dexterity and slowly disgorged its cargo of cars onto the quayside. A tall, bearded man in dirty blue overalls and a yellow safety jacket beckoned Jamie's car onto the ramp, which led into the ferry's cavernous hold. He pointed to the far end, where another smaller but similarly dressed man waved him into position with authoritative hand gestures. Other cars were manoeuvred alongside and behind him, until they were all packed in very closely like the proverbial sardines in a tin.

Jamie opened his car door a crack and managed to squeeze out. He was assaulted by the sharp tang of fumes and oil and the clang of metal. He helped Ellie out of the front passenger seat and then leant into the rear seat to lift the children out of their car seats. Other passengers were emerging stiffly from their vehicles. He held Georgie in his arms with Joe at his side, as Ellie rummaged in the boot for a bag of toys and books to keep the children entertained during the crossing. They followed a family up the dark metal stairs into the brightly lit lounge with tables and comfortable looking banquettes. Jamie picked a table which was next to the large expanse of windows but also near to the cafe bar. As the ferry began to chug away from the dock at a stately speed, Jamie, with Joe on his knee, watched the mainland slip away into the greying distance. Once they were out at sea, Jamie joined the queue at the bar and bought a glass of white wine for Ellie, orange juice cartons for himself and the children and a large bag of cheese flavoured tortilla chips.

He had always loved the romance of crossing the sea to reach his grandparents' island. As he gazed through the grainy, spray lashed windows, the waves marched implacably towards the distant line of the horizon, almost lost in the dull uniform greyness. The lack of colour did not dampen his quickening anticipation of reaching his island refuge, to which the throbbing forward motion of the boat gave momentum.

Joe's pestering to go on deck broke into his reverie. Ellie was already in the process of zipping up Joe's knee length anorak and pulling a woollen Beanie over his ears, notwithstanding his attempts to wriggle free.

'You little Bebe,' she said and playfully patted the end of his nose. 'It will be freezing and very windy out there. So keep yourself wrapped up'. She handed him over to Jamie and he caught the ghost of a smile hovering over her lips, which instantly brightened his own mood.

Jamie and Joe climbed the steps to the upper deck where Jamie had to struggle against the force of the wind to open the heavy door onto the deck. Jamie tightened his grip on Joe's hand as they ventured outside into the wind and the spray, which drenched them as soon as they emerged. The ferry was listing heavily in the swell and Jamie and Joe had great difficulty in keeping their balance. It was like climbing a slippery slope at a 45 degree angle but with a huge effort Jamie managed to haul Joe to the heaving rail, which they grasped like a life line.

'Let's go to the stern, where it will be less windy. Hold onto the rail and don't let go' Jamie shouted to Joe.

Clinging like limpets onto the rail, they slowly battled their way round to the stern where there was at least some respite from the wind. They stood together, for a moment, transfixed, as they watched the circling kittiwakes, fulmars and gulls ostentatiously flashing their wings tips, outperforming each other in a spectacular ballet of soars and swoops in the boat's wake. The ferry was passing a string of rocky outcrops, which looked as if they had been randomly hurled into the sea by a fractious giant. Jamie pointed out a basking colony of large grey seals with their long flat faces, large soulful eyes and sloping Roman noses; the bulls distinct in their thick rolls of flesh. When he saw the grey seals, Jamie knew that they were on the final approach to the island and shouted to Joe that they would be arriving soon.

They hurried to retrace their steps and rejoin Ellie and Georgie in the lounge, where they all sat and watched the shore of the island creeping closer and closer through the window. It was now possible to distinguish the individual crofts dotted on the hillsides.

The thudding engine began to change its rhythm to a slower tempo. A loudspeaker announced that the ferry would be docking in five minutes. This was the signal for the car passengers to gather together their belongings and make their way down into the hold to squeeze themselves back into their respective cars. There was a loud metallic clank as the ferry drew along the quayside and the engines juddered to a halt. Light flooded into the hold as the large bow doors were opened. Jamie's car was the third car to be ushered onto the metal ramp. His wheels jolted as they met the concrete of the landing stage. He always loved that jolt, as it was the first sign that he had arrived on Eilean na-h Fhadra. He followed the two cars ahead as they turned right onto the coastal road, a single track with passing places, which tightly hugged the edge of the island. The sun suddenly appeared like a miracle to turn the grey sea below him into glittering silver. As he drove along, he lowered his car window so that he could fill his lungs with the salty island air and hear the sharp cries of the sea gulls as they skimmed the lapping waves. He felt a glorious sense of release. He was finally throwing off the heavy cloak of anxiety which had enveloped him in its suffocating folds for so many days.

What he did not know was that the last vehicle off the ferry was a black car.

***

Finn had been as good as his word. The cottage was warm and welcoming as they arrived. Finn helped them carry their luggage including a travel cot over the dunes to the cottage. The luggage was abandoned once inside the bright red vestibule, as Ellie could not wait a second before having a short tour of the property. Ellie was not the kind of person who held on to her anger and her excitement at seeing the cottage soon dissipated any lingering anger she felt towards Jamie. Joe immediately ran to the plate glass window, excitedly shouting 'Look, everyone, at the sea'. Finn slipped into the kitchen, whilst Jamie was showing Ellie round, and emerged seconds later with a bottle of whisky and three glasses. With glasses in hand, they all joined Joe at the window to marvel at the dramatic beauty of Garvaay Bay. The bay was magnified under the louring winter sky, its gunmetal clouds billowing over a throbbing sea.

Watching the turbulence of an Atlantic storm whipping the waves into a frenzy of foam was an intoxicating experience for Joe. Next morning he was keen to walk along the beach with his father. They were buffeted by fierce winds, which caused their scarves to whip against their faces but the cold and the discomfort did not deter Joe from racing towards the waves and then retreating backwards as they threatened to flood his boots. Jamie loved to hear Joe's whoops of joy. Joe found a broken twig, which had been stripped bare by the sea, and Jamie helped him to trace his name in the sand with the stick. They stood together and watched as the waves crept closer and closer and finally washed his name away.

Ellie had fallen in love with the whole ambience of the cottage. She now understood why Lur Beag had such a romantic hold over Jamie. Although the kitchen was only tiny, she made some delicious, hearty Provencal soups, which she had learnt from her grandmother and which warmed up Jamie and Joe on their return from the beach.

Isla came round with her three children on the first afternoon. She brought a large tub of Lego bricks, which kept the children happily entertained. They built a large space station on the floor on which they landed tiny space craft. Joe named his space ship 'JG77'. Georgie sat on a cushion on the floor, entranced by the busy activity of the other children. Jamie was delighted to see that this time Joe was relaxed with Isla's three children and happily participated in their games.

Supper that evening was tarragon chicken followed by coconut ice cream. Jamie and Ellie celebrated with a bottle of white wine. When the children were in bed, they cuddled together on the sofa, gazing out to sea, and sipping from tumblers of whisky.

Jamie murmured in Ellie's ear 'This was a brilliant idea. I have never seen the children so happy'.

Ellie whispered 'This place is so magical, Jamie. Your grandfather was a genius.' She laughed softly 'Now I have seen Lur Beag, I may never want to leave'.

At first light the next morning Joe rushed in his pyjamas to the large window and gasped, when he saw that the ferocity of the waves overnight had covered half of the beach with a dense mass of bubbling foam. After breakfast the whole family wrapped up in their warmest coats, hats and scarves, donned Wellington boots and slithered down the dunes. Joe ran at full pelt through the foam, which floated and swirled around him. He picked up handfuls of foam which he tried to throw in the air but which disintegrated almost at once, leaving just a trace of sand on the palms of his hands. He then carefully gathered some of the foam in his cupped hands and ran to Georgie to show her his prize before it disappeared.

Jamie had his grandfather's binoculars and was scouring the sea. In the distance he caught sight of the pale grey wings of the black guillemot with its striking black and white plumage and distinctive red legs. He followed its powerful flight as it skimmed the waves before diving for fish and crustaceans below the sea surface.

'Look there' he shouted to Ellie and Joe over the boom of the wind. He pointed out to sea, 'It's a black guillemot. Can you see it?' They looked, but Joe was more intrigued by the foam which was constantly shifting along the beach in large drifts.

Jamie swung the binoculars round the bay and then turned with his back to the sea towards the hills above Lur Beag. Finn had told him that golden eagles had been seen on the island and Jamie longed to catch a sight of one. As he swept the binoculars up over the hillside, something glinting on the hill caught his eye. He took the binoculars away for a moment and peered with his naked eye. There was definitely something up there winking in the sun. He trained the binoculars on the spot and could make out the massive boulder which perched incongruously on the hillside, an erratic remnant of the Ice Age. He could just make out the black shape of a lone figure standing in the shelter of the boulder. The flashes of light came from binoculars, which were trained directly on Jamie. Jamie froze. Ellie, sensing something was wrong, waded through the foam to reach him.

'What is it?' she said.

Jamie pointed at the hill, 'There is someone up there watching us with binoculars. I am going to climb up and see who it is'.

Ellie cried out 'Don't be so paranoid, Jamie. This nonsense has really got to stop'.

Jamie was brusque 'I am sorry'.

Ellie's anger was about to burst into flames but he had already turned on his heel and was walking briskly towards the dunes.

On the steep hillside beyond the cottage was an ancient silver birch wood. The trees were stunted and had grown into distorted shapes due to the fierce winds which mercilessly raked the hillside. Thick tangles of ferns gathered in the open spaces between the trees which made climbing through the wood an exhausting exercise. Jamie found himself breathing hard. His chest was heaving painfully, as he fought his way through the ferns, which wantonly looped round his ankles as if their sole purpose was to delay him. He stumbled over a log which lay hidden in the thick of the ferns but managed to keep his footing. He stopped to catch his breath, bent over with his hands resting on each thigh. Suddenly there was a crashing sound to his left and he saw, for no more than a second, the rump of a disappearing deer.

As the trees began to clear, the hillside grew steeper and he had climb on his hands and knees until he emerged from the wood onto a narrow shelf of rough grass. He could now see towering above him the massive shape of the boulder. Although it looked as if one push would cause it to roll down the hill and crush him, he took comfort in the fact that it had stood on the hillside for millennia. He scanned the underside of the boulder but he could not see anyone standing there or nearby. He crept stealthily towards the boulder, but his ragged breathing would have given him away if there had been anyone there. When he reached the boulder, he scrambled all the way round it and then scoured the hill above it, but there was no one. He sat in front of the boulder, looking down towards the bay, where he had been happily with his family only minutes before. Had he imagined the figure? Was he seeing things that were not there? Was he going mad? Ellie clearly thought so and, if he was not careful, he would lose her. He laid back against the cold stone and closed his eyes, trying to steady his breathing and reassemble his scattered thoughts. He heard a rustling and opened his eyes quickly in fear, only to see a black pheasant strutting proudly through the long grass towards the edge of the birch wood. As his eyes followed the stately progress of the pheasant, he noticed something in the grass and scrambled to recover it. It was a protective cap for a binocular lens.

He pocketed the cap and later showed it to Ellie as proof. She was unimpressed, giving a Gallic shrug. She murmured that it was probably a local birdwatcher, adding that 'she could not understand why the Brits were so mad about birds. To the French they were only interesting when in a casserole'. She then looked at him, her chocolate eyes flashing with anger, and reproved him sharply 'Don't you dare run off and frighten the children again. They were having fun and you ruined it. You are always ruining everything'.

The magic spell of the island as a refuge had been broken for Jamie. He just wanted to pack up and go. This infuriated Ellie but she finally acquiesced because she could see that the holiday was now over for both of them. They returned to the leaden skies of Edinburgh with Jamie's anxiety heightened and Ellie's frustration mounting.

Joe's school nativity play began to loom high on the horizon. He had been chosen for the part of Joseph and was thrilled to be playing his namesake. His teacher, Mrs Sally Linton, telephoned, asking if he was better and likely to be there for the rehearsals. Ellie made it clear to Jamie that they could not disappoint Joe and that he had to return to school. She added that, if he thought it was necessary, he could take Joe to school in the morning and collect him in the afternoon. Previously they had shared this task and it was a sign that Ellie was losing patience with him over his fears. She was now openly telling him that they were irrational.

Sally Linton was a warm person with a bubbly personality, whose enthusiasm for a class room of boisterous five year old children was infectious. She was in her early forties with frizzy ginger hair framing a round, smiling face. Although she was short and very plump, which she tried to disguise unsuccessfully with loose floral dresses, she nevertheless dominated the room with her energy and chutzpah. Jamie was unsure as to what her reaction would be when he approached her to alert her to his worries about Joe. He thought she would dismiss him as paranoid like Ellie but she was surprisingly sympathetic and down to earth, promising to keep a watchful eye on Joe. She asked Jamie whether he had been to the Police and he told her about his frosty reception at the Police Station. This dispiriting experience, he said, had made him realise that it was up to him to ensure Joe's safety as best he could. He did not mention that Ellie thought he was being irrational and excessive.

Jamie and Ellie both attended the nativity play, which was scheduled at 4 pm on the Monday before the school broke up for the Christmas holidays. Jamie's mother had happily volunteered to baby sit for Georgie. His mother was always willing to help and had rallied from her earlier disappointment over the cancelled zoo trip.

They were early at the school hall, which doubled as an assembly and a theatre, and so were able to get seats in the front row, slightly to the left of the stage. Jamie had a digital video camera with him. Mrs Linton had gone to a great deal of trouble to obtain permission for Jamie to film the play. He was officially doing it for the school; the intention being to show the video to the children in the New Year. Jamie could hear the commanding voice of Mrs Linton over the babble of excited voices emanating from behind the red velvet curtains. Other parents were beginning to fill up the seats. Ellie waved at one of her friends, who was searching for a free chair. Jamie could not stop himself from scanning the faces of all the fathers, just to reassure himself that there were no unfamiliar faces.

When everyone was finally settled in a seat, the lights were dimmed. This was the signal for the chattering parents to fall silent. The curtains began to open slowly to reveal a tableau of Joe and his little friend, Morag, standing very still, dressed as Joseph and Mary with striped tea cloths bound round their heads. They were surrounded by a group of children, some dressed as shepherds and some as angels with cardboard wings. Suddenly one of the curtains got stuck. Mrs Linton swiftly marched onto the stage and tugged vigorously at the curtain to free it. The curtains were then closed again in front of the now giggling Joe and Morag. This set off a gentle ripple of amusement through the audience. The curtains reopened; this time with a flourish and without a hitch.

The play turned out to be a delight. All the young actors remembered their lines without too much prompting from Mrs Linton and the carols they sang were remarkably tuneful, given that the children were only five years old. The music teacher, Beryl Renfrew, who matched Sally Linton in her ample size, could be seen vigorously conducting the singing from the wings. The parents were loving it especially when little things went wrong such as the wobbling scenery, which three angels had to prop up to prevent it from falling down. Jamie was enjoying himself filming the whole event. It was proving a welcome distraction from his anxieties. As the children were taking their bows to thunderous applause, he went and stood to the left of the stage, turning his camera onto the enthusiastic audience, who were clapping wildly. As he swept the audience with his camera, his attention was caught by a figure lurking in the deepest shadow by the exit door. The figure was marked out by being the only person in the hall who was not applauding. A flood of horror coursed down Jamie's spine, causing him to shudder so violently that he had to lower the camera. He took a deep breath and forced himself to look again towards the dark corner, but the space by the exit door was empty.

As soon as they returned home, he blurted out to Ellie that he had seen the figure at the nativity play. Faced with her scepticism, he said that he would run the film and show her. She insisted that they should wait until the children were in bed. This took longer than usual as Joe was hyper-active after the excitement of the play. Ellie went upstairs to settle the children, whilst Jamie began downloading the file from his camera onto the computer. Neither of them was in the mood to enjoy a full rerun of the play. Their mutual pleasure during the play had dissipated during an evening of palpable tension between them. So Ellie sat there stony faced as Jamie fast forwarded to the final section of the film. He hovered over the computer ready to point out the shadowy figure to Ellie. The end of the film captured the first few rows of parents applauding with enthusiasm but the rear of the hall was so dark that it was impossible to make out any of the faces of the parents sitting towards the back. Just as the camera was pointing in the direction of the rear exit, Jamie had clearly jerked the camera. From that point onwards the film descended into a confusion of images. Ellie sighed deeply and then turned on Jamie, saying in exasperation 'For God's sake, stop being so paranoid. Just to let it go.'

***

Jamie could not let it go. Yes, there were times when he had real doubts about what he was seeing and what was happening to him. Ellie's reaction exacerbated those doubts. She was the most sympathetic person he knew and yet he had managed to anger her with his suspicions. But, were his suspicions paranoid, as she suggested? Was he being irrational? Was he obsessively sensing danger that did not exist? The big question which he returned to again and again was 'Should I ignore these feelings of threat?' Despite questioning his sanity over the last few weeks, he had to answer that question 'No'. Deep down inside him, he just knew that it would be a mistake to ignore his instincts, whatever the cost, and he feared that the cost may be his marriage.

There was something about the registration number of the black car which kept niggling away at him. He found himself sitting at his computer, ostensibly engaged in drawing a complex grid under the valley gutters of a roof section. However, in his mind he was playing over and over the letters 'QY 65 PBM'. There was a ghost of an idea almost within reach but he could not get it into focus. He found himself doodling boxes round the letters on a pad of paper which he kept beside the computer. He tried to snap out of his reverie and concentrate on the drawing on his computer. He liked the pleasing, geometric effect he was creating and began softly singing to himself a mantra of 'bad, mad and dangerous to know' to a tune he dredged up from an old Led Zeppelin song. Suddenly in the corner of his mind's eye, he caught a glimpse of the vivid oranges, blues and greens of a swirling poncho. Like a lightening rod this triggered a spark of memory, which he knew he could no longer ignore.

He sat bolt upright in his seat and cried out loud what he had known deep down for some time but had, for some Freudian reason, wilfully suppressed, 'Paul... My God, don't let it be Paul. It can't be his black car, can it? Surely he's...'

He instinctively grabbed his phone which was lying on the desk and googled the number for the Kelvin Infirmary, which he jotted down on a scrap of paper. He telephoned the number. After being left on hold for what felt like hours, he was eventually put through to the coma ward. The nurse was highly defensive to begin with but he sensed an instant thaw when she realised he was asking after Paul Minton.

'It was extraordinary,' she volunteered, 'He woke up just as if someone had switched on a light. I was there and what a shock it was when he opened his eyes. Others on my ward had experienced a patient waking up from a coma after months but it had never happened to me before. He was my first and it was a wonderful moment. He was obviously groggy and as weak as a kitten and he could no longer get his words out properly but he showed a remarkable mental resolve to get going again. He did so well physically that he was moved to the Rehabilitation Centre at Berry Hill. That would have been a several weeks ago but you may still find him there'.

Jamie thanked her and ended the call rather abruptly. He feverishly traced the telephone number of the rehabilitation centre. The receptionist there was maddeningly slow in providing any information due to a malfunctioning computer, of which she made complaint every ten seconds or so. Eventually she opened up the relevant file and, muttering something darkly about Data Protection, nevertheless confirmed that a Paul Minton had been a patient there but had discharged himself a couple of weeks before. Of course, that roughly coincided with when Jamie had his first sighting of the black car.

Jamie sat for a long while, as if paralysed in his chair, with his head bowed and both hands gripping his thighs to prevent himself from slipping forward into the chasm he felt opening up under him. A nightmarish inversion of Arvo's birch forests began pouring into his mind. The once tall, noble trees had become stunted, distorted and black, reflected in pools of putrid, green water. He could see, stretching to infinity, a desolate, war blasted scene of horror, across which was spattered a single gob of blood red spittle. He inwardly recoiled. This released a sufficient shot of adrenaline to break the spell, which had kept him pinned to his chair. Adrenaline galvanised him and he raced out of his study into the hallway where he swung back the front door. He stood in the doorway scanning the street from left to right and back again. With relief he could not see any sign of the black car amongst the parked cars.

He went back inside and closed the door. As he turned his back to the door to return to his study, he sensed again a dark brooding presence waiting for him just outside the door. Digging his nails into the palms of his hands, he resisted the temptation to fling back the door and look outside. He knew that that way madness lay.

As a means of calming himself down, he began to put together as methodically as he could the scattered fragments in his mind. He realised that at some level he had always known that his stalker was Paul, even though reason had kept telling him that he was in a coma in a hospital bed. For too long the deep sympathy he felt for Paul in the agony of his illness had clouded his own judgement and blunted the acuity of his insight. It had even caused him to question his premonitory terrors. Now recent events forced him to face up to the reality, however unpalatable. Paul was no longer the committed surgeon, the devoted husband but a man whose cruel disease had turned him into a dangerous stalker with a vendetta against his family. He could sense a black cloud hanging over his family, a harbinger of an oncoming storm, which only he could see. Jamie felt very alone with his fear.

It was a crisp, late afternoon, a pale sun fading intermittently behind a grey bank of cloud, when they set off for the German Christmas Market. Joe had missed going with a friend's family to this Christmas Fair, when they were at Lur Beag. So Ellie was insistent that they go as a family to make up for this loss. She reassured Jamie that Joe would be safe because he would be with them, stressing angrily that they could not spend their whole lives hiding away.

As Ellie still found the Scottish winters cold, she had enveloped herself in a puffer jacket and encased her feet in black, fur lined boots. She wore a red beret at a jaunty angle on her head. She was pushing Georgie's buggy at the front of their family convoy. Georgie's little, melon face peeped out from under the fetching Fair Isle pom-pom hat she was wearing. A cosy nest of blankets were tucked around her to keep her warm. Jamie and Joe in matching camouflage parkas were bringing up the rear; Jamie clinging tightly to Joe's hand.

As they crossed Princes Street at the corner of Hanover Street, they glimpsed the first of the wooden stalls with their red pitched roofs protruding beyond the steps to the Royal Academy.

The Alpine themed stalls crammed the concourse alongside the Royal Academy building and then sprawled on either side of the principal avenue in Prince's Street Gardens towards the Scott Memorial, which was temporarily dwarfed by the slowly revolving Big Wheel. The stalls' roofs were dressed in boughs of fake fir and red berries entwined with twinkling fairy lights. The inside of the stalls were lit with warm lights so as to cast an enticing glow over the many different types of wares, all clamouring to be sold. They included spicy scented candles, intricately carved wooden carousels and cuckoo clocks, snow globes, multi-coloured woollen scarves, hats and mittens, Arctic furry caps with large ear flaps. There were sparkly Christmas tree baubles of every conceivable hue and giant neon stars winking Christmas cheer.

There were food stalls with large loops of dark purple German sausages hanging from the rafters in dense thickets. Others displayed pretty gingerbread houses, the windows and doors picked out in fancy white icing. There were a number of stalls decked out as Bavarian bars with touches of pink and white gingham at Gothic style windows. They were selling foaming golden beer in oversized glasses and hefty shots of spiced glühwein in gold rimmed tumblers. There were sticky toffee apples, whirls of pink candy floss, glistening jewel coloured sweets, tiny striped candy canes and a magnificent chocolate fountain with dark voluptuous chocolate flowing over its tiered sides.

In the hollow lying below the main avenue there was a giant snowflake gateway festooned with flashing lights announcing the entrance to Reindeer Land. Inside a giant helter skelter commanded a scene crowded with all sorts of rides from the traditional carousel of prancing reindeer to pocket sized rockets flying to dizzying heights in the evening sky.

The tightly packed throng of people moved in a slow, shuffling dance along the avenue, mesmerised by the kaleidoscope of giddy, gaudy delights and seduced by the heady aromatic smells.

Jamie, Ellie and the children joined the tide flooding the avenue. Joe excitedly pointed at a stall on which a street scape had been constructed out gingerbread and populated by jelly baby people. Jamie lifted Joe up so that he could have a good view. Jamie was himself charmed by the mixture of architectural styles on display. In amongst the traditional Gothic style houses with ornate sugar work carvings, there were skyscrapers made of dark treacly gingerbread and boiled sweet windows, which glowed like stained glass windows where they were lit up within. There was even a sprinkling of what looked like brutalist buildings with caramel wafers replicating rough concrete. Polos were used as cladding on some of the buildings and desiccated coconut as pebble-dash on others. Seeds and nuts were used for a mosaic effect on domed roofs and candy canes looped together for doorways with tiny, green marzipan trees lining the street. Ellie was meanwhile busy buying a pair of rainbow striped gloves for Joe and red and blue spotted mittens for Georgie at the neighbouring stall.

Their next stop was at a stall displaying snow globes and Jamie could not resist buying one each for Joe and Georgie. He remembered marvelling at his grandmother's snow globe with its little sleigh pulled by the tiniest figures of reindeer across a snowy scene. He used to wonder how they were fixed inside. He spent hours shaking it up and down to create a snow storm, which obliterated the sleigh and deer with its dense, swirling flakes, and then he waited expectantly, as they slowly and magically reappeared.

Joe pulled his father towards one of the rides which was adjacent to the Scott Memorial. It had one seater capsules which looked like miniature bi-planes. They rose until they were at head height and then flew in a gently, undulating motion in time to Frank Sinatra's song 'Fly me to the moon' which was belting out into the concourse. Joe looked expectantly at his father, who initially shook his head and then relented with a smile. Jamie lifted him up and placed him carefully in the blue bi -plane. He told him to hang on tightly. He then stepped back and went to stand with Ellie and Georgie. The ride started off slowly and then gathered momentum until Joe was flying through the air. As he went round and round, Jamie never took his eyes off him. All too soon for Joe, the capsule floated downwards and came to a stop a little distance from where Jamie and Ellie were standing. Jamie jostled through the crowd to reach him. 'Can I go again' Joe pleaded and so Jamie paid the ride attendant, a leather faced man with long straggly hair, the money for a second ride.

As Jamie watched Joe's capsule begin to rise, he was distracted by a figure who was standing in the crowd on the far side of the ride. The figure was watching Joe. Jamie was not close enough to see his face clearly but the figure held him spellbound. It carried a deathly chill of loneliness, which marked him out from the throbbing, vibrant throng like a leper. That sense of raw horror, which had so unnerved Jamie before, now returned with stabbing violence. It grabbed him by the throat and almost choked him with the vomit of fear.

He could see that the ride was beginning its descent and that Joe's plane was going to come to a halt close to where the figure was standing. He began to run. The densely packed crowd impeded his progress. He began rudely pushing people aside. He was rammed by a child's buggy which the mother happened to wheel into his path. He had to wait for her to manoeuvre the buggy past him before he could continue on his headlong way. The ride had stopped and Jamie fought his way ruthlessly to the blue biplane. He clambered on to the ride and looked into the blue bi-plane. It was empty. He began running round the inside of the ride looking into each capsule until he was grabbed by the burly, tattooed attendant.

'Have you seen a little boy aged five with auburn hair' he gasped at the attendant 'He was in the blue plane'. The attendant shook his head and then forcefully told Jamie to get off the ride. Jamie jumped down and began running frantically to and fro through the crowd, first to the left of where he had seen the figure and then to the right. Joe was nowhere to be seen. Nor was there any sinister figure in the vicinity. There was just an endless stream of happy, chattering strangers. Jamie did not know what to do. He stood there paralysed and indecisive. He could not control the frantic wings of panic which were fluttering in his chest. Knives of dread pierced him deep in his stomach. He wanted to scream. He wanted to vomit.

Ellie had been watching Jamie's frenzied search through the crowds and realised that something must have happened. She pushed her way to where he was standing.

'Where's Joe?' she said.

'I don't know. I can't find him. He was snatched from the plane. I saw someone watching him before the ride finished. He's...disappeared,' Jamie answered bleakly.

'Oh, my God', she said. His fear was tangible and this time Ellie believed him. She put her hands to her mouth in horror, 'What are we going to do?'

Jamie's mind came back from a very dark place and jolted him into a semblance of action 'We need the police. It's hopeless trying to find him ourselves.'

They began to hurry back along the Avenue against the tide of shoppers. At the entrance to the fair, they spotted a hut with a couple of security guards cosily drinking tea inside. Jamie ran up to the hut and, with his head through the open door, yelled at the startled inmates that his son was lost and had been taken by a stranger and was in danger. Both guards immediately picked up on the urgency in Jamie's demeanour. The smaller of the two guards waved Jamie into the hut and asked for names and the details. The other larger, bearded guard put down his mug and got hold of his walkie talkie, which he began talking into in an animated manner. Within a few minutes two police officers, a grizzle haired older man with a neat moustache and a short, square shouldered young woman, arrived at the hut. Jamie repeated in a rush of fractured, desperate sentences how they had been menaced by a stalker for weeks and how the stalker had just snatched Joe and disappeared with him into the crowds. The male officer, PC Barry Doig, kept telling Jamie to be calm and to slow down, which Jamie found difficult as he felt time was slipping away from him and that he ought to be doing something rather than talking. He was cloyingly hot and sweat was running down his back. The female officer, PC Rona Mackie, was doing her best, meanwhile, to comfort Ellie who was by now weeping uncontrollably outside the hut. Georgie, who had woken up, was crying inconsolably in her buggy.

Suddenly Jamie's mobile phone began ringing. He felt oddly cold and began shivering as if he had just emerged from a lake of broken ice. His brain was now running on pure instinct. He fetched the phone out of his pocket and pressed the loudspeaker button. A man's voice could be heard. It was difficult to follow as the words were slurred. Jamie said 'Hush' urgently to the occupants of the hut and asked the telephone caller to repeat what he had said. There was something creepy about the voice which made them all stop what they were doing and listen intently.

'Joe came to me.' The speaker stressed the word 'me' and then continued in his lisping, barely audible tones 'We are together now, as it should be. We are soon going to go to sleep for ever, aren't we, Joe? We are going to make a big fire, aren't we? We are going to spread a huge orange glow across the sky like the fireworks at Hogmanay. You will like that, won't you Joe?'

Jamie shouted into his mobile phone 'For Christ's sake, what fire? What the hell are you talking about? Where's Joe?For God's sake, he's only five years old and you are frightening him. Please, please don't hurt him.'

The voice replied 'Watch and see, imposter' and then laughed unpleasantly, 'Watch the fire, Big Daddy'.

Before Jamie could say another word, the mobile phone went dead. There was silence in the hut, as everyone had been chilled by the menace in the voice. It was pure evil. They all felt it and involuntarily shivered. No-one questioned that the words carried some terrifying threat.

Jamie's mind went black momentarily before a livid, nightmarish hallucination of Joe screaming and beating his hands on the inside windows of a burning car was seared across his vision. His legs collapsed under him. He was caught by the male police officer as he stumbled forward. PC Doig said to him 'Come on laddie. What the hell is going on?'

Jamie could only whisper in absolute horror 'He's going to burn him, my Joe. He's going to burn him'.

The Officer shook him really hard 'You need to tell us what's going on. Who the hell was that creep?' PC Doig had been really rattled by what he had heard.

This brusque treatment had the desired effect of bringing Jamie to his senses. Only by forcibly swallowing back his hysteria was he able to get out the words 'The stalker, Paul Minton. He wants to kill himself and my son, Joe.'

The Officer spoke roughly to him 'Come on! I need details, any details you can give me about this Paul. Description, address, profession, car make, registration number anything'.

Jamie wiped his face with his hands to try and wash himself free of the horror and clear his mind.

'He drives a black car, registration number. Oh God, I can't remember the number. No, yes I can. QY...65 PBM. He's going to torch the car with...with Joe inside. Please believe me...'

He clutched at the Officer's uniform in his desperation, 'We have to find Joe. Paul is very very ill...has gone insane...wants to destroy my son. We have to stop him. Oh, my God, please, please stop him'.

PC Doig was already radioing Paul Minton's name and the registration of the car to headquarters.

***

PC Doig sat Jamie down in the hut and was trying to make him give a history. This was difficult as Jamie kept feverishly jumping up, shouting that they were wasting time and should be out there looking for Joe. The policewoman came into the hut and said that Ellie and the baby needed to get home. Ellie was ashen, shaking and clearly in shock. The two officers had a hurried conversation. A decision was taken that the family would be taken home straight away and the interview continued in the familiar surroundings of their home.

Their police vehicle was parked on Princes Street beyond the Scott Memorial. PC Mackie collapsed the buggy and stowed the wheels in the boot of the car. Jamie and Ellie sat in the rear, strapping Georgie between them in her buggy seat, which converted into a car seat. PC Doig could not turn the vehicle round and so drove along the length of Princes Street towards the West End.

Progress was slow due to random groups of shoppers, who kept stepping out onto the street for a moment's respite from the crowds milling about in dense packs on the pavement. Towards the end of Princes Street where the New Town shades into the West End, he turned right into Charlotte Street, passed alongside the Georgian town houses of Charlotte Square and descended down North Charlotte Street. He then took a right turn into the long sweep of Queen's Street. All the while the police radio was crackling with disembodied voices giving messages in snatches of half sentences. Jamie and Ellie sat in silence, their eyes staring into the far distance, sightless.

They were travelling past the Gothic red sandstone edifice of the National Portrait Gallery along York Place towards its junction with Broughton Street. A message blared out from the radio which shattered abruptly the tomb like atmosphere inside the car.

'A black car reported careering erratically off Queen's Drive. Said to be mounting the pedestrian path leading up to Hunter's Bog. Cars, Charlie Tango 439 & Bravo Wilko 337, to the scene. Chopper on its way' said a voice with a thick, gravelly accent.

'That's us' said PC Doig grimly. Over his shoulder he said to Jamie 'Have to go. Can't take you home'.

Jamie had snapped out of his lethargy. Adrenaline was now pumping through his system. He cried out 'For Christ's sake, just hurry'.

PC Mackie immediately activated the police siren and the vehicle's flashing lights. The wailing sound was instantly deafening inside the vehicle, as the police car began accelerating, dodging and weaving past those vehicles ahead which were too slow to get out of the way. At the top of Leith Walk, with wheels squealing, the car shot round the roundabout onto Leopold Place on the London Road. Jamie and Ellie were thrown sideways at the back of the car, straining their shoulders against the seat belts. Jamie instinctively leant forward to put his arms protectively over Georgie.

PC Doig shouted back 'Sorry. Hang on in there.'

They sped down London Road at about 70 mph, several cars mounting the pavement to give them precedence. At Easter Road they turned right and, in the absence of any traffic, gained further speed They climbed Easter Road with the high stone wall on the right and crossed Regent Street before descending Abbey Mount. The vehicle swept under the railway bridge, past Queen Mary's Bathhouse, an ancient stone building jutting into the road on the left, and the tall grey tenement buildings dominating on the right. The vehicle swivelled over the tiny roundabout into Horse Wynd with the House of Holyrood Palace on the left. The Palace was subtly illuminated to showcase the drama of its ancient turrets against the black night sky and, probably, to shame the jarring modernity of its neighbour, the Scottish Parliament, across the road. All of this was lost on the occupants of the police car as it slowed to take the sharply angled bends which were moulded round the outer walls of the Palace. Turning left at the small roundabout, they finally drove onto Queen's Drive at the point where the Radical Road starts its ascent, scoured into the precipitous face of Salisbury Craggs. They could now hear other sirens wailing in the distance.

Just beyond where the ice cream van stands in the summer, the pedestrian path was just visible in the light cast by one of the Park's lamps. It shimmered like a narrow grey ribbon winding its way up and around the bottom edge of Salisbury Craggs until it disappeared out of sight into the darkness of Hunter's Bog, the marshy valley between the towering point of Arthur's Seat and the tilted, sweeping back of Salisbury Craggs. The police car swung onto the path. It was not wide enough for the vehicle's wheels and all four wheels began to slither in the soft turf. For a moment it looked as if they were not getting any purchase on the ground. The Officer put his foot off the accelerator. There was just enough momentum for the wheels to gain some traction and the vehicle jolted awkwardly up along the path.

It slewed round the corner into the blackness of Hunter's Bog and crawled along the sliver of tarmac until the tarmac gave way to a narrower dirt track. In the distance was a clump of trees, swaying like silver ghosts, on either side of the track, signalling that the way ahead was impassable for vehicles. Seeing this knot of trees in the headlights, PC Doig swung the vehicle violently to his right and began ascending the steep slope diagonally alongside some gorse bushes, where the rough grass was shorter. The vehicle was struggling up the slope, the engine grinding horribly and the wheels desperately skittering and swivelling. Jamie could see to his right the lights of Meadow Bank and beyond that, of

Leith, twinkling far below him.

Half way up the slope the headlights picked out a narrow track to the left, which ran parallel to the crest of the Craggs. PC Doig swerved onto the track only for the engine to conk out and the vehicle to come to a juddering halt. PC Mackie began radioing their position and reporting what she could see.

Jamie looked out of the passenger window at the wide swathe of Salisbury Craggs whose rear slope rose above him at a vertiginous angle. He felt like a sailor watching the massive back of a killer whale rear out of the waves, a sea monster, just a few yards away from his flimsy vessel. Near the top of the incline, just below the huddle of rocks at the very edge, he saw the black car. It was parked at an angle with the headlights on full beam. The four doors were open and the interior light was spilling out onto the surrounding grass. The car CD was blaring out at full volume Verdi's Requiem. A figure was stumbling round the vehicle with something in his hands. Jamie realised it was a petrol can. Crying out to the officers 'He's got a can of petrol', he sprang out of the rear passenger door and, before either officer had time to remonstrate, he began sprinting up the slope towards the black car. The figure could see him but carried on mechanically sloshing petrol round the wheels of the car.

As he neared the figure, Jamie began yelling to make himself heard over the music. 'Please don't do this, Paul. He's only a child. You are a good man, Paul, but you are ill and need help. We can get you help...'.

Jamie then in his desperation played the gamble of his life. He shouted as loudly as he could, 'You do not have to destroy the child's life. He's my biological son, not yours. He carries no curse, do you hear me? No curse'

He could not know whether he was exacerbating an already volatile situation. He was working on raw adrenalin. There was no time to think. Paul hesitated for a moment but then turned to look at Jamie with an unblinking stare.

Jamie was close enough to the black car to see that Joe was lying motionless and unresponsive on the back seat.

'What have you done to him?' Jamie screamed.

He grabbed hold of Paul and began shaking him. He felt Paul go physically very weak. His head lolled like a doll without any stuffing. He stumbled to his knees, spilling petrol over both of them. He said something but his words were drowned out by the music from the car CD. Jamie bent over him and managed to to catch the words 'It's a sleeping draught...so he won't be frightened.'

Jamie was engulfed with rage at what was happening to his son and he gave Paul a savage push backwards. Leaving Paul spread-eagled on his back, he ran to the open rear door of the car. He was leaning in to pick up the sleeping figure of Joe when he was grabbed round the neck. Paul was shrieking like a mad man and suddenly from nowhere had the strength of ten in his hands, which he used to apply a strangulating pressure on Jamie's throat. He dragged him out of the car. Jamie could not breathe and in his panic was desperately clawing at the tightening grip on his throat.

Suddenly a helicopter rose over the lip of the crag with an overpowering throbbing noise. The wind from its whirling blades buffeted the car and the two men struggling alongside it. Its searing search light raked the ground and temporarily blinded both of them. Jamie seized the moment to throw all his weight backwards against Paul. The surprise caused Paul to relinquish his hands as he found himself falling backwards with Jamie on top of him. Jamie, still choking, got to his feet and plunged back towards the rear door of the car. This time he succeeded in sweeping his limp child into his arms.

As he turned he saw that Paul was standing and was fumbling in his coat pocket. He looked straight at Jamie, his face distorted by a look of pure hatred. He shouted at him 'You can't win. Look at how Joe came to me at the Fair, to me...his father.' He stressed those last words. He then produced from his pocket a box of matches, which he waved triumphantly in Jamie's face. Jamie realised to his horror that Paul's illness had so completely destroyed the last vestiges of his sanity that he was insensible to all rational entreaty. The gentle doctor had become an automaton operating on the fuel of an irrational hatred.

'I want to die but you don't, Jamie McHugh. Fear makes you weak...'

He had picked up the empty petrol can and laughed, as he turned it upside down and not a drop fell out. He started to open the box of matches. Jamie began to run carrying Joe over his shoulder.

'Go on, run away but the taint of the fire is already on you' came the mocking response.

The slope was too steep and Jamie found he was losing his footing. The urgency to get away was overmastering but he was going to fall headlong and jeopardise Joe, if he continued to run downhill. He could hear Paul's piercing laughter over and above the music. Jamie looked back and saw that Paul was now feverishly striking match after match. Jamie threw himself to the ground and, clinging onto Joe, began to slither on his bottom down the slope, frantically pumping his legs. He was made all too aware that, in the proximity of the fire, he was wearing petrol soaked clothes which could spell death for Joe and himself.

Behind him he heard the whoosh of a fire igniting into frenzied, crackling life. He could not help himself. He had to look back again. He saw to his horror, Paul, with flames beginning to dance round him, settling himself calmly into the driving seat of the car. The 'Dies Irae' was still streaming at top volume out of the vehicle. Jamie gasped and part of him wanted to run back and drag Paul out of the car but knew he could do nothing now to help him. He also knew that the last thing Paul wanted was his help. Paul wanted to die. Jamie just sent up a prayer that his clothes were not leaving a trail for the hungry flames to track and follow him like a ribbon of lava. He slithered onwards into the dark recesses of the hill.

His descent was arrested by the arms of the two police officers, who had been creeping up the hill to provide assistance, notwithstanding their orders to wait for reinforcements.

'We've got to hurry. It's going to explode' said PC Doig.

Jamie could hear high pitched screams over and above the last rites of the music, as the unrelenting flames devoured human flesh. He closed his eyes and prayed as hard as he could that it would be over soon for Paul. There was a terrible smell of burning material and mini metallic explosions were erupting at an accelerating rate. Gouts of fire were gushing out of the vehicle and flames spurting through the windows of the car. The heat was intense and hot air surged towards them.

They only just reached the Police car, as the whole sky filled with explosion, as if Armageddon was raging. Metal was extruded in vitriolic fury far and wide. They huddled, crouched by the side of the police vehicle with their backs to the blaze. Mercifully the shrapnel detonated by the explosion failed to reach the area of the police car. Other police cars were now arriving together with a paramedic van. Sirens were blazing and flash lights were blinking crazily.

Against this chaotic and cacophonous backdrop, Jamie, with Joe over his shoulder, and Ellie, with Georgie in her arms, watched the ravenous flames spiral into the night sky. The flames had generated a lurid haze which hung suspended like a vast veil over the whole ridge. The eerie orange Valhalla glow would have been visible for miles over the city scape of Edinburgh.

www.ingramcontent.com/pod-product-compliance
Lightning Source LLC
LaVergne TN
LVHW051004080826
845145LV00009B/2446

* 9 7 8 1 7 3 8 4 8 8 0 1 8 *